A BRIDE FOR HEDDWYN

SONGBIRD JUNCTION
BOOK TWO

JACQUI NELSON

Cover design by Marlin

ISBN eBook: 978-0-9958596-8-5
ISBN Print: 978-1-7773113-1-5

PRAISE FOR THE SONGBIRD JUNCTION SERIES...

A Bride for Brynmor
Songbird Junction, Colorado - January 1877

"A special journey that kept me following along to see what would happen. I cannot wait to read about the other two sisters and also Brynmor's brothers turn out!" ~ Lori D.

"A perfectly written love story." ~ SKM

"Oh, I love this book. There is something about getting lost for a few hours in this era. So well written and descriptive, you feel like you are right there in all the action." ~ B

"A great love story with perilous danger." ~ Dorothy R.

A Bride for Heddwyn
Songbird Junction, Colorado - January 1877

"A splendid cast of characters...a book that will be re-read over and over again." ~ Crystal Crossings

I loved this couple. Heddwyn is perfect for Oriole and she for him." ~ Cheryl P.

"Throw in a cute puppy, a troop of gypsies, & meddling family, and the charming adventure is complete" ~ Michelle R.

"Mayhem, both funny and heart warming." ~ Betty R.

DEDICATION

For Glenda Young-Kinard and Pam Potter, two beautiful spirits who brightened many of my days—and the days of many others as well.

CHAPTER 1

January 1878
Denver, Colorado

The church bells rang for Lark and her husband, but they'd never ring for Oriole. Unlike her sister, Oriole couldn't depend on love, and no one could depend on her. All she could do was run from her past and present, which included the dangerously distracting Welshman who kept glancing over his shoulder and insisting they needed to talk.

About what he'd yet to say. She wasn't waiting to find out.

Leaving was her best way to save her other sister, Wren.

She must escape the wedding party departing the chapel. In the midst of these six different and not always harmonious voices, her silence grated the loudest. She didn't belong. She was out of tune. Stretched too tight. A strum away from breaking her row in their four-string procession.

First came the newlyweds, followed by the groom's sister

and her husband, then the groom's two brothers, and finally her—held in check by the arms of two well-meaning but meddling old-timers. Mrs. Fitzgerald mistakenly believed she was Oriole's grandmother, while Gus Peregrine insisted everyone call him grandpa whether they were related or not.

Little white lies and full-out falsehoods. They grew like weeds. Around her and inside her. When they'd met at the missionary orphanage, Lark and Wren told her their recently deceased mothers were Cree and their fathers were Irish fur traders they'd never met. She'd yearned for sisters. Being different made most people shun her, so she'd assigned herself the same history.

One of her first lies in a long list.

A sudden gust kicked up snow in her face. A reminder that today's mild-for-January weather could turn at any time.

"Horsefeathers," Gus muttered as he struggled to keep his beloved flat cap on his head and his ample beard out of his mouth. "Can't wait to move this shindig inside."

When Oriole clutched his elbow to steady him, Mrs. Fitzgerald patted her hand. *She thinks I need help as well.* The grande dame hadn't stopped giving orders since Oriole entered the lady's music shop a week ago, searching for Lark and Wren.

"Our celebration needs a *céilí.* And you, my dearest, must play for us. We're all eager to hear your violin."

"It's not mine." She strove to squash the waver in her voice. She longed to hold the instrument. How could she not? It'd been part of her life for more years than not. "The violin is yours now." *Or at least it is until I find Wren.*

The shop owner shook her head so vigorously her expertly styled—and controlled—cloud of white hair appeared in danger of falling. "Fiddlesticks. You cannot turn your back on your birthright or your talent."

"No one has to do anything if they don't want to." Brynmor's verdict rang loud and clear from the front of the line.

When Lark thanked him, Oriole silently did as well. Her sister was in excellent hands now. For this, Oriole admired Brynmor. And abhorred him too. He hadn't set out to end their tight-knit sisterhood, but he had.

She now had nothing but her quest to find Wren, while Lark had...everything.

Lark held fast to her husband and the gift he'd given her a few hours ago—Lark's favorite instrument, a hurdy-gurdy. "It's been a long day. All I want is to rest before we catch the train home."

Home. What an odd word. Neither of them had used it except in vague reference to the area where they'd been born, the Qu'Appelle Valley far to the north. Lark and Wren had always spoken fondly of their mothers and their households. So, Oriole had done the same. Another lie.

Lark's new home was Songbird Junction, a tiny train stop on the line to the mountain mining town of Noelle— where the couple who walked behind Lark and Brynmor lived.

"I'm keen to get home too." Max Peregrine kissed the crown of his wife's curly red hair.

"And back to work," Robyn teased with an easy smile that shone the brightest for her husband. "You never stop."

"That's because I get to spend my days working with my wife and my nights—"

Robyn's laughter and her palm pressed over Max's mouth cut him off. They'd wed on Christmas Day and now ran the Noelle freight office. An equal partnership made possible because after the Llewellyn siblings' parents died, the three brothers had raised their sister to work with them as wagon drivers.

Heddwyn and Griffin completed the line, walking behind Robyn and in front of Oriole.

"Livin' so far apart is foolish," Griffin snapped. "I'm only toleratin' it 'cause it might help us find Wren."

Although Griffin was the youngest of the Llewellyn brothers, he was also the biggest and the only one with a temper that he struggled to control. She hoped Wren never had to go near him because her tiny sister would be terrified of a gruff giant like Griffin.

"Lark and I will search the area around Songbird Junction," Brynmor said.

Robyn nodded. "Max and I will do the same in Noelle."

"Best get a move on then," Heddwyn added in a rush. "And get where we all need goin'."

Despite the conversation, everyone continued to behave in a maddeningly laid-back manner, except for the man who'd had the last word.

Heddwyn Llewellyn. The charming but scatterbrained brother, whose mesmerizing blue eyes she strove to avoid. He could never keep out of other people's business or stay still. He kept running his hands over his closely cropped auburn hair or his clean-shaven jaw—every time he glanced at her, the damsel in distress.

The charity case he'd only recently promised Lark he'd help. When they'd met two years ago in Cheyenne, he'd watched Oriole for different reasons.

Fickle man. You have a soul even less dependable than mine.

Last week, she'd been embarrassingly surly with Lark, who deserved only sweetness. She had to leave before she cracked completely. She stopped tracking Heddwyn from the corner of her eye and focused on what lay ahead.

No one else did. Griffin scowled at the ground, lost in his own turmoil. The couples now conversed privately. Even Mrs. Fitzgerald and Gus had struck up a conversation around her, like she wasn't even there, like she'd already gone.

The Denver freight office was close now. As soon as they reached it, she'd find an excuse to run to her wagon parked in the alley behind Mrs. Fitzgerald's Music Emporium. Then she'd drive out alone in search of Wren. And never see Heddwyn Llewellyn again.

The thought made her yearn to look at him one last time. Another reason to put distance between them. *He doesn't care about you. He has no idea who you are. He's never had the fortitude to look deeper and find out.*

She snuck a peek at him.

The flare of his wickedly gorgeous grin made her cheeks burn as he said, "I've always wanted to say your eyes are—"

"Stop staring," she hissed, then stiffened at her foolishness. When she'd said the same on their last day together in Cheyenne, they'd quarreled.

One of their remarkably few conversations. He was charming with everyone but her.

"I hate being stared at," she muttered as she struggled to keep her own gaze off him and on what lay ahead—the freight office where they'd part ways.

Above the last building between her and the Llewellyns' office, a charcoal cloud rose along with a crackling sound. Her gaze shot back to Heddwyn.

"Turn around," she urged, "and *look* at the fire ahead of us."

He spun in a blur and sprinted away even faster. Gus and Mrs. Fitzgerald's arms around hers prevented her from following.

Loss, then fear, stabbed her heart. "Be careful!" Her shrillness made her cringe.

Luckily, her outburst came at the same time everyone, including Lark, stopped talking and chased after Heddwyn. She feared only for her sister. Another lie for her list.

She held her elderly companions close and hustled them forward as fast as she could. When they rounded the corner, the heat stole her breath.

Flames covered the side of the barn closest to the office. The wedding procession formed a new row, grabbing buckets, shovels, boxes, and even a few planks of wood to toss snow on the blaze. She couldn't drag a grandmother and grandfather into that fray.

The elderly pair suffered no hesitation about dragging her. Straight into the office where they thrust any object that could carry snow into her arms. Next, they pulled her back outside to distribute the lot to the many townsfolk—including Sheriff Guyette—who'd arrived to help.

"We're in this together," Mrs. Fitzgerald proclaimed.

Gus winked at the lady. "We make a darned good team."

Her team had always been her sisters. Their trio against the world.

Where was Lark?

She raced toward the growing line of people. Her ebony-haired sister, sandwiched between a pair of redheads, was hardly recognizable. Ash covered this new trio's heads. She shoved her way between Lark and Griffin, earning a scowl and then a curt nod from him.

She put all of her energy into throwing snow onto the fire, which blazed even higher.

"I can't lose him." Lark's voice rasped worse than when Ulysses had choked her for disobedience. Tears streaked her soot-covered face.

The smoke and heat had Oriole struggling to speak as well. "Who?"

"Hedd won't let anything happen to Bryn," Robyn shouted.

"Where are—?" Her heart skipped a beat.

They weren't in the line.

On the other side of Robyn, Max caught her gaze and thrust his chin toward the barn. "They're freeing the livestock."

A hazy figure leading three blindfolded horses broke through the smoke filling the barn door. When he whipped off the cloths covering the steeds' eyes, they surged forward, and he released them. The horses galloped down the street. The man ran back inside the barn.

"Wait!" Had that been Heddwyn? Would that be the last time she saw him? The possibility hurt like a kick in the gut. She turned to Robyn, then to Griffin. "Why aren't you with your brothers? Why aren't we all—?"

"They gave us orders," Robyn yelled as she continued tossing buckets of snow. "We fight the fire. We give them more time."

Griffin muttered words only she could hear. "We also keep Lark from going in after Bryn. He'd never forgive us if something happened to her. Hedd told me to watch over you too."

"Me? But he doesn't—"

A wave of smoke, whipped by the wind, hit her. Seared her throat. Left her coughing. Choking. Unable to breathe.

She yanked Lark down with her. Crouching where the air was only slightly better, they renewed their efforts to extinguish the fire. How much worse would it be inside the barn?

Why hadn't Heddwyn and Brynmor come out?

As if sensing her question, Lark's fingers clutched hers tight. When Oriole raised her head to meet the obsidian gaze she adored, she flinched.

Lark's fathomlessly deep and determined eyes were now dull with misery. "They're looking for our lambs."

"Lambs? What lambs?"

"We couldn't leave them at home. We worried we might not make it *back*"—Lark's voice broke on a sob—"in time to feed them."

"Both you and Bryn will see Songbird Junction tonight." With surprisingly gentle hands, Griffin pulled Oriole and Lark to their feet. "Hedd will make sure of it."

Robyn and Max rose with them, swaying like specters fighting to stay above ground—or the ash that weighed them all down.

The one thing that remained firm was Robyn's tone. "In chaos, Hedd's the most dependable of us."

Griffin snorted. "It's the only time he's steadfast."

The Llewellyns' strength of conviction about their middle brother's dependability stunned her. She couldn't have heard right. The hellish inferno had fried her senses.

Heddwyn's family commented on his erratic behavior more than anyone. Most times teasingly. Sometimes woefully. He may be the same size as Brynmor and only a hand shorter than Griffin, but he seemed light in comparison, like a child who'd never grown up. He couldn't—

Her heart leapt when she glimpsed a shape striding out of the barn. A large man hunched under someone of equal mass slung over his shoulder.

Their group surged forward as one to help him. They didn't have to. He moved fast and only set down his cargo when they were a safe distance from the blaze.

The moment he did, Lark flung her arms around the

man on the ground. When he opened his arms to do the same, the two balls of singed wool he'd held so close Oriole hadn't noticed until now, started bleating and tried to bolt.

She grabbed the one closest to her. The man who'd saved Brynmor did the same.

When Heddwyn's sky-blue gaze met hers, she couldn't look away. From a face as dirty as hers felt, his smile shone brighter than ever. Until he lowered his gaze and murmured soothing words to the lamb now cradled in his arms, like he didn't want either of them to run away from him.

She hugged her lamb to stop herself from grabbing hold of Heddwyn and never letting go.

Robyn embraced her brothers wholeheartedly, then shook her finger at Heddwyn like a disapproving schoolmarm. "What happened to you being the fastest?"

"Yeah, *Peaceful*." Griffin arched a challenging brow as he stressed Heddwyn's nickname derived from *blessed peace*, the meaning of his Welsh name. "What took you so long?"

Heddwyn gestured to Brynmor sitting on the ground. "*Big Hill* was too large to reach the back of the crate his pets were hiding in."

"You couldn't either," Brynmor grunted.

"True," Heddwyn shot back with a grin. "But I was the one who caught 'em when they finally darted out."

Brynmor sighed. "The truth is, you're now faster *and* stronger than me."

A frown replaced Heddwyn's good humor. "No, I can't be. You just need a few more days to recover from getting shot." His teasing smile returned as quickly as it had departed. "Or you got lazy and faked taking a nap to make me carry you."

"How can you joke about this? You could've died." Oriole's outburst turned the Llewellyns' joyful reunion into a grim silence. From the corner of her eye, she saw Heddwyn watching her closely again. She faced her sister. "And it would've been our—" She swallowed the word *fault*.

Worrying about Heddwyn was an unfamiliar sensation for her, but Lark had feared for Brynmor's well-being for too long. She pressed her lips tight. Making Lark feel guilty again was out of the question.

But Lark refused to let Oriole hide behind anyone's silence, her own or the Llewellyns'. "Why do you suspect Ulysses is responsible for the fire?"

Behind the crowd that had gathered around them, the barn shuddered and collapsed. No one had been hurt. Not physically. But pain came in many forms. She didn't want to say another word that caused Lark more anguish.

Plus, the fire hadn't changed what she must do. It only made her certain that she must do it faster. Like Heddwyn. *Stop thinking about him. Leave everyone and find Wren.*

She transferred her lamb into Lark's arms. "An unattended lantern might've started the fire."

Heddwyn gave his lamb to Brynmor. "We're too careful for that. And your troupe manager is in jail, so why do you think he's involved?" He took a step closer to her.

She refused to take one back. She couldn't let him know how much his nearness affected her. She must treat him like the crowd. She bristled under their gazes. *One day I'll find a place where no one stares at me.*

Today, however, was not that day.

She raised her chin and scanned the townsfolk for the man she'd glimpsed earlier. She steeled herself for everyone's scorn as she pointed at him. "Because he's here."

"Of— Of course I am," Sheriff Guyette sputtered. "When I received word of the fire, I ran to help."

"And that leaves *who* guarding Ulysses in jail?"

The sheriff stiffened as if she'd slapped him with an offense. "My deputy, of course."

"He's either a bought man or a dead man." She shivered, thinking of Ulysses' capabilities and his cruelties.

"Now see here," the sheriff huffed, "you've no right to malign a man's character like this. Deputy Nash is trustworthy. He comes from a good background."

Meaning she couldn't be trusted because of hers.

"Help!" A man ran toward them. Blood dripped from a small cut on his temple to the tin star on his jacket. The deputy skidded to a halt in front of his superior. "The prisoner has escaped."

"How in tarnation did that happen, Nash?" the sheriff demanded.

"After you left, armed men stormed the jail. They overpowered me."

"The fire was a distraction." When Sheriff Guyette's gaze found her, Deputy Nash's did as well.

"You were wise to be suspicious." Heddwyn rocked on his heels, like he wanted to spring forward but was forcing himself to stand still. Or at least in one spot.

"Yes! Everyone knows they"—the deputy thrust his finger at her and then Lark—"will get us all killed."

"No, you will." Griffin seized the man by his shirtfront and shook him like a rag doll. "*You* let the lunatic who almost killed my brother escape."

Heddwyn leapt forward. Robyn joined him. They each grabbed one of Griffin's hands and pried open his fingers. As soon as they did, Heddwyn shoved Deputy Nash away from them with enough vigor to put him on the ground.

Nash crawled behind his boss. "Ulysses T. Stone has vowed that anyone who keeps him from his women will burn in Hades."

"Shut your big bazoo," the sheriff hissed. "You're making a terrible situation worse."

A tremor of fearful voices swept the crowd, fracturing it and sending the townsfolk scurrying to their homes. Heddwyn started pacing.

"You're not *his women*. You're free, and we'll make sure you stay that way." Despite her words, Mrs. Fitzgerald's arm once again twined around Oriole's and held her close. "Mr. Peregrine, I was glad to have your assistance today."

Gus nodded solemnly. "We work well together, Mrs. Fitzgerald."

"Agreed, but now we must part ways. You'll travel with Brynmor and Lark to Songbird Junction, then continue to your home in Noelle. Oriole and I will return to my shop."

Heddwyn halted his pacing to stand beside her. "I'll go with you."

Her thoughts raced for the best reason he shouldn't. There were several beyond her need to be on her own. Gus was notorious for wandering off alone—mostly because he forgot where he was going. His family would never let him travel from Songbird Junction to Noelle unattended.

Max and Robyn would accompany Gus the entire way home, and Heddwyn would have to stay with Griffin.

Robyn reached for her husband's hand. "You must go with Grandpa Gus."

Max pulled her into a hug. "And you must stay with Griffin, so Heddwyn can help Oriole."

No, that must not happen. Before she could voice her objection, Griffin did.

"No one has to stay with me," he snarled. "Go where you need to go. I'm gonna see that the office is secure." He stomped off.

This time Brynmor's sigh was heavy with regret. "Griff

has every right to be angry. There's too much work to do here, and we're always finding more elsewhere."

"I'll talk to him about hiring someone to help us," Robyn said.

That would take time. And there was Oriole's answer. "Until you do, who'll have the time to retrieve the horses you freed from your barn?"

Heddwyn groaned. "I'd forgotten about them."

Lark whispered something to Brynmor as she helped him climb to his feet.

He nodded. "We'll stay in Denver and help."

No, that wouldn't do. She strove to keep her voice indifferent. "You'll miss the train."

Heddwyn threw his hands in the air. "Who will tend Songbird Junction's water tower and pumphouse tonight? You just got them functional, Bryn. You need to protect that investment and your new life. Sheriff Guyette, can you—?"

The lawman halted him with both palms raised. "Slow down, son. I'm no good at running after horses, but I can escort Mrs. Fitzgerald home and stay with her for *one hour*. I'll not shirk my other duties." He scowled at Oriole and his deputy before heading toward the music shop. "I have a prisoner to recapture."

The sheriff's pride had saved her. He'd given her an hour to leave town without being seen. She followed him as swiftly as her combined pace with Mrs. Fitzgerald—who still held her arm—allowed.

Heddwyn joined them, shortening his long stride to match hers. "I'll see you very soon."

No, you won't. She sealed her lips to stop herself from announcing her victory.

"I'll stable the horses at the livery near Mrs. Fitzgerald's. If I hurry, I'll see you in less than an hour."

Not if I hurry as well. She kept her gaze fixed on the sheriff, whom they'd almost caught up with.

"Then we can finally talk," Heddwyn added.

"I have nothing to say to you!" Another lie. But at least she hadn't yelled the truth. She wanted to scream at him for making her continually crave something she'd never wanted until she met him.

Mrs. Fitzgerald nudged Heddwyn in the ribs with her elbow. "If *you* want to say something, boyo, best say it now."

"It'd take days to say everything." He drew in a deep breath, then blurted, "Because that's how long Oriole and I have known each other while almost never speaking to each other." His breath heated her cheek as he bent his head and whispered close to her ear. "I want to talk about what happened after we kissed."

CHAPTER 2

Two years earlier...
January 1876
Cheyenne, Wyoming

"You've finally gone too far, Peaceful." Despite his reprimand, Griffin's face appeared annoyingly composed, without a hint of the flush that rose with his notorious temper. Only his blazing red hair matched the meaning of his name in Welsh.

Heddwyn latched onto his brother's nickname like a drowning man, cringing even before he uttered his lackluster reply. "You think so, Ruddy?"

Tonight had been a complete disaster.

He'd lost his wit and his will to sit up straight. He dropped his head onto his arms on the table. The music had ended. The performers had left the room. The Crimson Theater no longer contained anything worth seeing.

"Tell me something I don't already know, Griff."

"If she hadn't slapped you, I would've."

"I know that, too."

From his chair on the other side of the table, Griffin heaved a sigh that sounded a lot like Brynmor's.

Big Hill and Little Red not witnessing Heddwyn's disgrace was the one bright spot in tonight's catastrophe. That, and the fact that for all his bluntness Griffin would never utter a word to anyone about tonight. He'd leave that to Heddwyn.

His younger brother's ability to keep a secret didn't prevent him from needling the person about it. "I'm sorry you can't have what you want."

He jumped to his feet. "You make me sound like a child."

Griffin crossed his arms and leaned back in his seat to stare up at him. "You don't need me for that, but you need to accept the truth." A frown finally cracked his brother's calm. "There's a woman who may never like you the way...you like her."

"But—" Heddwyn groaned as he collapsed back onto his chair. "At last, she was looking at me with those amazing eyes. Just me. Like there was no one else in the room. And then I couldn't..." He waved his hands in the air, wishing he'd kept them to himself.

"You couldn't stop yourself." Griffin shrugged. "You never can."

"This was different. *She's* different. I need to talk to her." He strained to see the back door where Oriole and her sisters had departed. And entered. Where he'd been standing when she walked in, looked at him, and he... couldn't stop himself.

"Why didn't you apologize right away?"

"Because..." He still hoped he could fix things *if* he could find the right words.

"Because you were too busy staring at her again?"

"*Because* saying I'm sorry might give her the wrong impression."

Griffin snorted. "You're daft."

"I don't want her to think I made a mistake."

"But you did."

"*But* I'll never regret kissing her. I only wish I hadn't done it in such a rush."

"Or in front of a crowd. You've put ideas in their heads."

A ripple of unease tensed his muscles. "How so?"

Griffin gestured to the room full of men. "They're probably thinking of doing what you did."

"They most definitely should not!" He shot to his feet again. The thought of anyone touching Oriole made his blood boil.

"You need to blow off some steam. Let's take a walk." Griffin dragged him outside.

When they faced the gloom of the street, he couldn't stop glancing back at the lantern-lit theater in search of Oriole. Movement in the alley caught his eye. In the moonlight, a shapely silhouette walked toward him, holding something that looked like a violin. When a cloud cloaked the moon, the figure vanished in the shadows.

Had she actually been there? Or had his eyes summoned the vision he craved?

Griffin's gaze was elsewhere. He stared toward their boardinghouse. No matter how humble or temporary, his brother was happiest at home with his entire family around him.

He'd been happy there as well. But never content. *Now I know why.* "I'm going back inside the theater."

Griffin swung to face him. "No, Peaceful, you're not. Believe me. When your temper's rising, you should not—"

"I'm *not* like you."

"Fine," Griffin snarled, then shoved Heddwyn so hard that he staggered. "Go fight with strangers. But remember, you have family depending on you. We've spent years keeping Rob and each other safe. Don't ruin that in one night."

Heddwyn paced in a circle, glancing between the alley and Griffin stomping away from him. *Ruddy's wrong. I often make a muddle of things, but I more often than not fix them.*

He sprinted into the alley. The clouds moved again, and the moonlight revealed...nothing.

From the shadows came a voice. "Where are you going in such a rush?"

His feet skidded to a halt, but his heartbeat sped up. He knew that voice. Every night for a week, he'd listened to its owner sing in perfect harmony with two others. But he'd never heard her speak. Not even after he'd tasted her lips.

Oriole stepped out of the dark. In the shifting light, she reminded him even less of the vibrant but unvarying songbird she'd been named after. Her eyes were as changeable as amber gemstones circled by a stormy blue.

She raised her chin at an angle directed away from him, as if to challenge and escape his appraisal at the same time.

He'd made a dismal first impression. *Stop wasting your chance to fix that. Answer her question.* "I needed to find you so we could talk."

"From what I've seen, you talk too much." Her reply dried up his words, but his fingers came alive, twitching to touch her.

That had been his first mistake in the theater. He'd touched her hair, then his hand had somehow slipped around the back of her neck and drawn her close for their kiss.

She raised her violin between them. "Can you hold on to this for me? With both hands and only for a moment."

The way she glanced from him to the ends of the alley—like she was uncertain about all three points—made him hesitate. "What's wrong? Why...only for a moment?"

"Because that's how long I told my sisters I'd be gone."

As soon as he took her violin, she took his elbow and pulled him into the shadows. The pitch dark swallowed him and everything near him.

His eyes strained to see her and failed. "Oriole, I—"

"If you say anything, I'm leaving." Her other hand grasped his shirtfront and turned him in a half circle.

When his back hit a wall, he almost lost his grip on her violin, an instrument he'd yet to see her not holding. He cradled the precious parcel against his chest. "Say anything about what?"

"For starters, our kiss."

"That cat's out of the bag. An entire room of men saw." He shifted his weight from one foot to the other, straining to see more than her silhouette against the moonlit alley behind her.

"Is that your biggest concern?"

He shook his head before realizing she probably saw less of him than he could see of her. "I shouldn't have grabbed you the way I did."

"That's why you're holding my violin right now."

"It is?" He ran his fingers over the smooth wood, wishing it were her hand. He yearned to pull her closer.

"You can never stand still." Her hands covered his, holding him motionless as the warmth of her body came closer, until the instrument seemed to be the only thing separating them.

"How do you know that I—? You've been watching me."

He couldn't contain his grin. All the time he'd stared at her, he'd never seen her look his way. "I should've waited for a private moment and—"

"Stopped talking?" Her lips brushed his, soft as a butterfly in flight.

"Oriole," he whispered her name in reverence and amazement.

"Please *stop talking*."

"But I need to tell you—"

She halted him with her lips.

Her mouth stole his breath. Swiftly. Then slowly. The perfection of both spiked his pulse. Impossible. Incredible. Each kiss better than the last. "How are you doing this?"

Who'd taught her? She didn't wear a wedding ring or a whore's rouge. She smiled sweetly at everyone, sang like a siren, and played the violin like a hellion. But he'd never seen her encourage any man's advances. The memory of her slap still stung his cheek.

And he'd yet to apologize.

When he spoke, he kissed her between his words. Never more eager to do two things at once. "I need to—tell you—I'm—"

"Don't," she replied in the same way. "Don't ruin—this. Until you—came along—I—needed nothing."

"That—can't be true."

Her flinch left him bereft of her lips. "You think I'm lying?"

"I think everyone needs something." He wanted to be the one to give her everything life had to offer. "Tell me what you need, Oriole."

Her hands left his and tried to take the violin away from him too. "I can't trust you."

He held tight to the instrument, his one link to her. "Why not?"

"I shouldn't be doing this." She stepped back, dragging her violin—and him still holding it—with her.

"Wait."

"No, I'm too reckless. *You're* too reckless. And nosy. Why couldn't you be quiet and just kiss me for one moment?"

"Give me another chance. Give me another...moment." He bowed his head to touch hers and released her violin.

She didn't move. Neither did he. They stood in silence. The only sound was their ragged breathing. Strident. Out of tune. Until one of the perfectly smooth sides of her violin bumped his hand.

No, it nudged his hand.

When he took hold of the instrument, their lips met instinctively. He kissed her the same way she kissed him. Without seeing. Without speaking. Without asking for anything more than the moment.

CHAPTER 3

January 1878
Denver, Colorado

*H*unching his shoulders against the chill wind gusting down his coat collar, Heddwyn closed the livery door and jogged to catch up with Griffin. "How can life go so right and so wrong at the same time?"

Instead of answering, his brother increased his pace toward their next destination. They headed even farther away from their family.

With their lambs and each other held close, Brynmor and Lark were on their way back to Songbird Junction. But Grandpa Gus had refused to go home to Noelle. The stubborn rascal and his equally tenacious grandson had stayed with Robyn at the Denver office. Max had started the business, so it couldn't be in better hands, especially with Rob by his side.

Why couldn't Oriole have wanted to stand by him like that?

Waves of jealously tore at his happiness to see his sister

and brother so well matched. He lengthened his stride, trying to outrun his demons and keep up with whatever ones drove Griffin.

With their siblings and workplace secure, Griffin had insisted on helping him. Between the two of them and a bucket of oats, catching and stabling the horses had scarcely taken thirty minutes. Mrs. Fitzgerald's Music Emporium was now in sight.

His heart beat like a clock on a countdown.

In a minute, he'd talk to Oriole about all the things they'd never discussed. Except for their kissing. No use mentioning that. *That* was ancient history.

"I'm done living for the moment."

"If you say so," Griffin muttered, his temper now on simmer.

"I'm also done holding my tongue."

"Wasn't aware you ever did."

Their easy banter, even when disagreeing, made him laugh. "You're the perfect example of the right and the wrong at the same time." He clasped Griff's shoulder.

His brother shrugged off his hold. "Just saying something doesn't make it true."

"Exactly." He pulled his brother into a hug.

Griffin went still as a mountain. "What're you doing?"

"I'm thanking you." *While I have the chance.* He released his brother and crossed the final distance to the music shop.

Griffin followed him. "For what?"

"For talking to me, even when you're angry with me."

"I'm only annoyed we almost lost you in a fire."

"If you say so." Heddwyn froze with his foot on the front step of Mrs. Fitzgerald's music shop. His confidence gained from bantering with Griffin vanished. He didn't merely want to talk to Oriole. He wanted her to talk to him.

What could he say that would interest her?

He'd had hundreds of conversations in this shop since his family had come to Denver and rented the accommodations upstairs. Chatting with their landlady had been easy. Mrs. Fitzgerald wanted to hear everyone's stories, even if they were reports of workdays.

He strained for a glimpse of Oriole inside.

All he saw was Sheriff Guyette, standing guard near the window with rows of musical instruments behind him. Oriole was in there somewhere. So was her violin.

She'd given it to Mrs. Fitzgerald because the lady had reason to believe it'd been her son's. The violin Oriole had taken everywhere. The violin she'd made him hold—so he couldn't hold her—every time they'd kissed.

Griffin heaved a sigh. "You'd better not be thinking about hugging me again. It's enough that Rob does that all the time now."

"Lark said Oriole had her violin when they first met at the orphanage." Without it between them, would things get better or worse?

"What if music is the key to everything?"

Bewilderment left him gaping at his brother's hushed but hopeful question. They'd traveled many roads together, but they'd seldom shared the same viewpoint.

Griffin stared at the shop, nodding as if he'd found his answer. "I'll stay with Mrs. Fitzgerald. Then the sheriff can search for Ulysses, and you can talk to Oriole."

Heddwyn adjusted his collar against another gust of wind. "That may take a while."

"I can use the time to learn about an instrument."

"Which one?"

Griffin arched a challenging eyebrow. "The mandolin, of course."

Surprise made his jaw drop. "That's Wren's favorite."

"*Really?*" Griffin replied sarcastically. "I never noticed."

"Are you saying—?"

"That I'm gonna do everything I can to help Wren. She may still come here."

Three weeks ago, while fleeing their troupe manager, the three sisters had agreed to meet at this shop if they became separated. Only Oriole and Lark had made it. Wren was too timid and tiny to fare well on her own.

"She's tougher than you think." Griffin's growl vibrated with admiration.

Surprised again, Heddwyn blurted, "You spoke with her in Cheyenne?"

Griffin fixed his gaze on the shop. "Have you ever seen Wren talk to anyone but Lark and Oriole?"

He hadn't, but he remembered Griff saying, *You need to accept the truth...there's a woman who may never like you the way you like her.*

His brother had been talking about both of them, while he'd focused only on himself.

Squirming with self-reproach for not paying attention, he tapped first one toe then the other against the step to knock the snow from his boots. "I'm sorry."

"Don't be. I never believed I'd keep Wren in my life. I just wanted to *keep her safe*. I still do."

Heddwyn wanted more for Griffin. He wanted him to be as happy as Brynmor and Lark. And Robyn and Max. "What if you could—?"

"No. I can't. So, save your words for Oriole."

"What if I say the wrong thing?"

"Then you're one step closer to finding the right thing. But try not to stare at her so much. Had no idea it made her that uncomfortable."

"Neither did I." How long had Oriole kept this secret? Was it why she'd only kissed him in the dark?

"I've never known you to hesitate." Griffin climbed the steps to the veranda. When Heddwyn jumped to follow, Griff added in a conspirator's whisper, "Remember, don't stare, but don't let her out of your sight either."

His steps faltered. "How can I do both?"

Griffin opened the door and shoved him through. "Stay near her," his brother hissed as he closed the door behind them.

The swiftness of their entry earned a nod of approval from the shop owner. She'd give anyone an earful if they hovered in her doorway, letting the warmth out. After the chill outside, the temperature inside enveloped him like a summer day.

With her sleeves rolled up, Mrs. Fitzgerald stoked the stove under several pots of steaming water. The industrious lady had already scrubbed her arms to her elbows and her face to her hairline. Anything further would require letting down her hair. A sight he'd never seen.

His landlady kept her appearance like her shop, painstakingly fixed to her standards.

Sheriff Guyette was another matter. He looked like he'd dunked his entire head in a washpot. His hair stuck out like an irate porcupine.

Had Oriole washed as well? An image of her dark-brown hair—and then her entire body—wet and glistening from her bath invaded his head. Sweat beaded his brow as he scanned the room in search of her.

Don't stare. Say smart stuff. Stay close to her. He liked the last part best. Any excuse to be near Oriole was—

"She's not here." Horror-struck by that revelation, he turned to Mrs. Fitzgerald, seeking an explanation.

She gestured to the back of her shop. "Oriole's in my bedroom resting."

That news eased his worries, but only for a second. "Why? Isn't she feeling well? Was she hurt in the fire?"

"She said she was tired." Mrs. Fitzgerald frowned. "With Lark living elsewhere and my devil of a nephew on the loose again, I told Oriole that sleeping in her wagon was now out of the question."

"Ladies do not live in wagons." Sheriff Guyette grabbed his coat and hat. "I did my job. I'm leaving."

Good. Heddwyn swallowed the urge to snarl at the man's narrow-mindedness but couldn't stop his feet from circling the room.

Oriole was a lady. So was his sister, and she'd spent most of her life on or around wagons. If that was a fault, it was solely his and his brothers'. They hadn't had many luxuries while raising Rob, but they'd never had to live in a box atop a wagon.

They'd also never mysteriously come into the possession of a caravan previously owned by travelers. Oriole had called them the Roma. In the few stories his father had shared about the old country, they'd been called a lot worse.

Mrs. Fitzgerald scowled at the sheriff's departing back. "My objections center on safety. And for once, Oriole didn't argue with me. She agreed to rest in my room."

"She lied. And ladies never—" Guyette flinched as Heddwyn's pacing brought them close enough for their equally irritated gazes to clash. Apprehension widened the man's eyes before he ducked his head. "You'll find out soon enough," he muttered as he fumbled to open the door.

Heddwyn slammed his palm against it. "What aren't you telling us?"

The sheriff tugged futilely on the door latch. "I only did what I said I'd do."

"What *didn't* you do?" Griffin growled, his face getting redder by the second.

"I said nothing when I saw her coming back with a horse."

"Back? What are you talking about?" Mrs. Fitzgerald shook her head. "Oriole hasn't left."

Guyette folded his arms. "I've no idea how she got out without me seeing."

Heddwyn pressed his hand against the door to stop himself from seizing the sheriff and shaking him as wildly as Griffin had shaken the man's deputy less than an hour ago. "You spent so much time staring out the front windows, you forgot about the ones in the back."

Guyette raised his chin. "Ladies do not climb out of windows."

"Stop spouting rubbish," Mrs. Fitzgerald ordered. "Why didn't you tell me Oriole had gone?"

"Because my deputy was right concerning one thing. Our town is better off without the likes of her." Guyette's words spilled out, gaining speed and conviction. "She isn't a lady. She's a heathen in every way."

Heddwyn's punch fell short of its target. Only Griffin's ironclad grip on his arm stopped him from silencing the man's vile mouth.

"N-now see here," the sheriff sputtered. "If she wants to leave Denver, we shouldn't stop her."

"Oriole can go wherever she wants." He twisted free of his brother's hold and sprinted toward the back door. "I'm not stopping her."

"Then why freeze your backside off chasing after her?" Sheriff Guyette hollered.

"If you don't do the same, pursuing the prisoner you lost,"—he shot back as he raced down the hall—"there'll be hell to pay."

If any harm came to Oriole, or her family, or his, he'd be going straight to hell. But maybe this time he wasn't too late. Maybe Oriole was still in the alley, hitching her horse to her wagon.

He flung open the door. A swath of blinding white destroyed his hope. Only a flurry of boot and hoof prints marked the snow, along with a pair of wheel tracks heading north.

Oriole had left without a word of warning. The same way he'd left her in Cheyenne. He hadn't planned that. He'd never had time for plans.

But back then, they'd both had their families to help pick up the pieces when others' plans crumbled. Or Ulysses Stone crushed them.

Now Brynmor and Lark were together. Wren was lost. And Oriole had gone looking for her on her own.

"Not for long." His vow left a ghostly trail in the air before disappearing in another gust of wind. "I'll find you."

CHAPTER 4

*O*riole suppressed her shout of triumph as her wagon finally passed the last building on the edge of Denver and left behind the traffic clogging the road. Instead, she focused on snapping the lines and urging her mare to pick up her pace. If she could get over the next rise, she'd be out of sight. Heddwyn might look for her in town. He wouldn't search further afield. Not in the farmland or the open range beyond.

He's not that interested in talking to you. He has more reason than ever to be distracted.

After recognizing his voice amid the commotion of horses arriving at the livery, she'd barely gotten her mare out the back undetected. How he'd arrived that quickly, she hadn't a clue. She'd cursed his uncanny speed. And prayed for her own.

With her horse in tow, she'd flown straight back to Mrs. Fitzgerald's. Hitching her wagon, a task she could've accomplished with her eyes closed, had been as swift as the next leg of her escape. North along the alley. Onto a busy thoroughfare. Losing her tracks among all the others. Heading west.

Life in a musical troupe controlled by a crooked manager had introduced her to many things, including how to make a getaway. Always try to blend in. Never steal something unless you're willing to kill the person who might come after it.

With the last of the money she'd taken from Ulysses, she'd purchased the most common horse. Brown and as unremarkable as her own hair. The wind kept trouncing her attempts to keep her hood in place and hide even her hair's plainness.

Such is life. One cannot control the weather. Or expect to succeed at everything.

Even Ulysses suffered setbacks. The last had been unprecedented. Arrest and confinement in jail for an entire week. Now he was out there somewhere, seeking to bind her and her sisters to him again.

When her wagon reached the top of the rise, an extra load of challenges hunched her shoulders. She'd run into Ulysses or his hired men before she saw Heddwyn again. She'd finally left her distracting Welshman behind. Safe, or at least safer, without her near him.

She forced herself to focus on what lay ahead.

The brief stretch of road before the next hill. The long expanse of snowbound fields on either side. Nothing looked out of the ordinary. Except for her mare's ears flicking back, listening to something behind her wagon. The rattle and creak of the round-topped box—that she barely had to stoop under when standing inside it—was now a hindrance as well as a blessing.

She edged sideways on her seat. She also pulled her hood forward, once again trying to shield herself from the rising wind and whatever followed. *You can't hide. Look before you lose the chance.*

She drew in a quick breath before glancing around the wagon and back the way she'd come.

A man ran toward her. Tall. Broad-shouldered. Covered in a dusting of gray ash. A strong silhouette against the snow. When her wagon rolled down the slope, he disappeared from sight.

He could've been any number of men from the fire. He wasn't. They'd spent too much time moving from moonlight to shadows for her not to recognize him. Even while running, he'd been adjusting the straps of the pack on his back.

Her breath left her in a tumult of emotions. Relief. Happiness. Disbelief.

Heddwyn was carrying enough to suggest he'd planned to be gone a while. His footsteps crunching the snow became their own tune. Clearer, louder, until he slowed to walk beside her.

"Where are we going to look for Wren first?" He was barely puffing after his run.

The ease with which he moved forward vexed her.

"There is no we." She glared at him from the corner of her eye. "You have to go back to Denver."

"No, I don't." He contemplated her mare as if she were extraordinary.

"How could you leave Mrs. Fitzgerald on her own?" She cringed at doing the same.

To better control Oriole and her sisters, Ulysses had lied and labeled himself their only living relative. But locked in jail where he couldn't hide from Mrs. Fitzgerald's direct gaze, she'd recognized him as her long-lost nephew. She'd shone a light on a past Ulysses had tried to bury. That, plus helping Oriole and Lark, made for two *burn in Hades* offenses.

Sheriff Guyette had promised to guard the music shop for one hour. That hour was over.

"Don't worry." Heddwyn's tone was calm but not calming. "Griff's with Mrs. Fitzgerald."

"Then Robyn's on her own." She couldn't believe Heddwyn or any of his brothers would allow that after the fire and Ulysses' escape.

He studied her wagon now. The most unique thing about it was that the door was directly behind her. One had to stand on the driver's seat to enter or exit the living quarters. Heddwyn didn't look at the door or anywhere near where she sat.

His sudden disinterest in looking at her frustrated her as much as her inability to make him leave her.

"Grandpa Gus wouldn't go home. He and Max are with Rob at our freight office."

And that had allowed Griffin to help Heddwyn gather their horses. That was how he'd arrived at the livery so fast. She couldn't move another inch forward until he went back. She pulled her wagon to a halt.

Heddwyn stopped with her. "We should visit all the farmhouses. I've made deliveries to some. I'll introduce you." He prodded the snow first with one toe, then the other, unable as usual to stand in one place.

The tapping of her own foot made her grimace. She forced herself to sit still and scour her brain for a reply while Heddwyn's words continued to flow easily.

"If the wind keeps picking up, it'll be a blustery night. Good thing I brought a warm blanket and a tent. I'll have the perfect vantage point to guard your wagon."

She had no other recourse. She pulled the note from her

pocket and held it out to him. "I found this wedged in the door of my wagon."

He took the paper, looking only at her hand and not letting their fingers touch.

Get over it. He's no longer interested in you in the same way. Plus, he'd never, except for their first kiss, taken anything she hadn't offered. Explicitly and brazenly. She'd acted like her mother. She was the one who couldn't stop herself from dragging Heddwyn into the dark and—

His voice, reading the note, yanked her out of the past.

"Travel alone or there will be grave consequences."

"Grave consequences?" Heddwyn snorted. "That's as overblown as him using the name Tombstone. He's more likely to find himself in a grave and under a tombstone than putting anyone else there."

"You don't know everything." But he'd known who'd written the unsigned note. He hadn't had to ask.

"Nothing you or Ulysses T. Stone can say will make me leave. Not even if you told me—" He waved his hands in the air. "I'm a horrible kisser."

The careening shift in their conversation made her spin on her seat to face him. His startled eyes met hers. For barely a second. His gaze fell to his feet, now planted firmly in the snow.

"Saying something so obviously a lie is useless." She prayed the cold would mute her blush. "Why must you be so difficult?"

"Why must you?" His voice was free of accusation but full of need, as if he desperately longed to know why.

"Because nothing between us has ever been easy." After every kiss, she'd wanted to talk to him. To be more than a woman and a man in the dark. To have a conversation about everything and nothing, the way she'd heard Lark and Brynmor do in Cheyenne. Every time she couldn't do that, she'd become angry. With herself.

If she hadn't lied so often, could things have been different?

"Are you—?" Heddwyn paused to clear the gruffness from his voice. He didn't succeed. "Are you prepared for a life all alone on the road?"

"Since Ulysses started controlling me by saying he was my uncle, I've been on the road more days than not." She didn't comment on the alone part. Heddwyn knew she'd been with her sisters from the moment their trio had met at the orphanage until they were separated fleeing Ulysses a few weeks ago.

"What are you going to say to the people you meet out here?"

"The truth. *I'm looking for my sister. Have you seen her?*"

"Why are you looking for her?" The question came from the road in front of them.

When she flinched, she jerked the reins and startled her mare as well. She mumbled soothing words to steady the horse and herself.

She'd been so lost in their quarrel, she hadn't noticed the rider's arrival. Who was he, and how much had he heard?

He didn't carry a gun. At least not openly. He had large hands better suited to a plow than a pistol, wore a coat with many patches, and rode a horse as plain as hers. He didn't look like a hired gunman, but every second she delayed answering him made his frown deepen.

"Because she's my sister."

He leaned his arms on his saddle horn, as if he wasn't

going anywhere soon. "I meant, why do you *have* to look for her? How did you lose her?"

The how haunted her. If she told him, he wouldn't give her the time of day. The night they'd fled Ulysses, they'd hidden on a rum runner's wagon and had to jump off unexpectedly. She'd lost her hold on Wren and her violin. If she'd reached for what mattered most, instead of scrambling to retrieve the instrument, Wren would still be with her.

"How's your wife doing, Ike?" Heddwyn's question flustered Oriole as much as the man's arrival. He knew him well enough to use his first name.

Ike's interrogation ended in a flash as he returned Heddwyn's smile. "She's better. Glad to hear your brother's also on the mend."

Heddwyn's smile waned. "You heard about the man who shot him?"

"Was told his name is Ulysses Stone."

Heddwyn gestured to her. "This is Oriole. Stone is looking for her sister, Wren. We need to find her before he does."

Ike cocked his head, studying her again. "You have odd names, you and your sister."

She'd been told that before and had always ignored the comment. She could never think of a decent response. Today was no different.

Ike glanced at the horizon behind him. "My neighbor spotted gypsies in the rangeland last week. You one of them?"

Heddwyn replied before she could. "She's Métis."

Where had he learned that word? She hadn't told him anything about her heritage, but Lark would've shared hers with Brynmor. Heddwyn, being nosy, had most likely questioned his brother and her sister.

"What's…Métis?" Ike asked.

She didn't think him hearing that she was a mixture of Cree and Irish would help. "It means I'm odd."

"It does not." Heddwyn's huff was indignant. "You're just different, like me. And our names are no stranger than Ike's wife's."

Ike chuckled. "Marigold would agree with you." He kept smiling when he met her gaze. "What does your sister look like?"

The simple question combined with his friendly expression loosened her tongue. "She's tiny, has light-brown eyes and hair, and doesn't talk. Or at least she won't talk to you."

Ike's smile faltered, as if he thought she was a hundred times odder than a moment ago.

She searched for something mundane to add. "When I last saw her, she wore a blue dress."

He nodded slowly. "My wife likes that color. She also talks so much I can't imagine the opposite."

"If you see someone fitting Wren's description, will you let us know?" Heddwyn asked.

Oriole gritted her teeth against objecting to his continued use of the word *us* and waited for Ike's response.

"I will."

She sighed in relief before blurting, "Don't tell Denver's deputy."

"Or the sheriff," Heddwyn added.

"Why?" she asked at the same time as Ike.

"I no longer trust either of them to protect you or your sisters." Heddwyn's growl of a reply sounded a lot like Griffin's when his anger spiked.

She felt her eyes widen along with Ike's. His in disbelief. Hers in astonished certainty. Heddwyn must've learned that

Sheriff Guyette had not only seen her leave, but been more than content to let her go.

Ike released a lengthy breath as he sat straight in his saddle again. "Well, you Llewellyns never gave me a reason not to trust you, so I'll do as you ask." He tipped his hat to Heddwyn and her. "Stay close to him, Miss. He'll keep you safe." He grimaced. "But first you'd better find a place to wash before you ask more questions. You both look a fright, like you fell into a chimney."

Ike reined his horse around them and continued on to town.

"See?" Heddwyn puffed out his chest. "Folks in Denver know I'm trustworthy. That'll help me help you. And Wren, too."

Oriole snapped her reins, setting her wagon in motion again. "He wasn't from Denver. That town is behind us."

Heddwyn smiled as he followed her, while once again not looking at her. "You said *us*."

She tucked her chin close to her chest and angled her face away from him and his persistence—and the blasted wind that also wasn't easing.

A shiver shook her. A frigid night sleeping outside would force Heddwyn to go home. She just had to be hard-hearted enough to leave him out in the cold. If she didn't, he might never make it back to his family. She'd burn in her own private hell if she let that happen.

CHAPTER 5

$\mathcal{U}$nable to start a fire in the wind, Heddwyn worked in the dark, stacking his gear inside his tent to prevent it from blowing away. He also wolfed down a cold dinner of beef jerky and day-old and darned hard biscuits. Another dreary addition to his new dining routine this past week.

Brynmor had always been the chef in their family. When Robyn moved to Noelle, their ritual of sitting together to eat after each workday had splintered. Then Brynmor went to Songbird Junction, and it'd been severed. Now he and Griffin ate whenever and whatever, saying it saved time for more work.

When he'd sprinted up the music shop's steps to their lodging above, the room had felt empty without Robyn and Brynmor's belongings. He'd stuffed his packsack full of food, blankets, and a change of clothes. The last thing he'd grabbed was the revolver he'd bought after Ulysses shot Brynmor.

The weight of the pistol carried memories. Mam had been a crack shot. She'd taught them about firearms and everything else. She'd anticipated doing the same with her fourth child. When death stole her before she could, Da had shot himself, and Bryn had refused to have a gun in their home.

The gun wasn't the problem. What it stood for was. The easy way out.

Da hadn't stayed and helped shoulder the weight of their soul-crushing sorrow.

For years, he'd hated him for that betrayal. Then life forced him to face his own shortcomings. Not directly, of course. Shifting tracks was his way to remain upright. That and helping Bryn and Griff raise Little Red.

The year Robyn turned twelve, they'd shown her the basics with a borrowed weapon before telling her how their parents died. Better to know *everything* than to live in ignorance or fear. Mam's rule and now theirs. They'd also taught Robyn loads of other ways to defend herself, so a gun wouldn't be the first thing she reached for. Now here he was, packing a Colt Peacemaker in a shoulder holster under his coat. The fastest hiding place he could reach.

The tent pressed in on him like a coffin. Maybe he'd welcome the snug fit later when he slept, enveloped in his own body heat. Right now, he needed to move.

He needed to ensure Oriole stayed safe.

Outside the tent, he paused only to secure the flap against the snow blowing in. He hiked the perimeter of the camp, squinting into the dusk and the biting wind, straining to see anything moving across the snow. The chances of someone finding them tonight were slim.

That didn't mean he'd stop looking.

After halting at two farmhouses and receiving more comments about their grimy appearance than about their search for Wren, Oriole had chosen to make camp. Her horse dozed beside a thicket of evergreens barely large enough to provide a windbreak and conceal them from the road. She'd covered the mare with a blanket, fed her oats from a feedbox on the wagon, gathered an armful of kindling and a bucket of snow, and gone inside her sanctuary.

Smoke puffed from its narrow smokestack. Light glowed behind its curtained windows.

Oriole was probably having a proper dinner or taking a bath. The one he'd imagined her having at the music shop. His skin grew hot. The storm no longer chilled him.

The lonesome howl of a coyote rose above the wind. Wisps of clouds drifted across the stars while the trees swayed gently. The squall had retreated. Now the rising moon could take center stage and begin its dance with the heavens.

Same as the night he and Oriole first kissed.

Thinking about that would be his best way to stay warm until he saw her again. That wouldn't be until morning when she came out to continue her search for Wren. He wouldn't get a chance to see Oriole's hair wet and glistening in the moonlight.

His one chance was to make himself useful. Oriole didn't need help with her horse or wagon. She was a seasoned traveler. He must find other ways to become indispensable.

Her wagon door squeaked open. Oriole stood framed in the light of a lantern behind her. The curve of her hip and waist made his mouth go dry.

"Why aren't you wearing your coat?"

"Because I won't be outside for long." She climbed down the wagon's three-rung stepladder as quickly as he came toward her. Streaks of light glinted in her wet hair like shooting stars that granted wishes.

I want you. Only you. When he raised his hand to catch his wish, Oriole raised hers as well.

She held a bucket between them. Water sloshed in it. "I'm just throwing this out and gathering fresh snow to melt for my mare to drink."

"Let me do that." His hand closed over hers on the handle. Mistakenly. Or maybe not.

If he'd wanted to ensure he grabbed the bucket, he would've looked at it and not her. And now...it was too late. Her eyes held him captive. They glowed like sunflowers in a summer sky. She gazed up at him as if he was the sun, and she craved him as much as he craved her.

There were no buildings casting shadows. No disapproving glares forced them to hide. They stood alone in the wide-open wilderness.

A tremor shook Oriole's hand as she swayed toward him.

"You're cold." He used his body to shield her from what remained of the wind.

The clean scent and sleek weight of her hair drew him closer. As did the softness of her skin. Her pulse raced under his fingertips. Her eyes widened, but she didn't look away.

Neither did he. He didn't want to miss a moment of staring into her eyes. Besides, he didn't need to look to know that the curve of her neck rested perfectly in his—

His gaze plummeted to his hand cradling the back of her neck. Oriole had only stayed close to him because he'd grabbed hold of her again.

He released her immediately. "Sorry. I vowed to never do that again."

The light in her eyes vanished. "You don't have to apologize for not wanting to do what we used to do."

Blasted words. He'd said the wrong ones. Nothing new

there. Time to take Griff's advice and keep talking till he found the right ones.

"I'm only sorry I rush everything and can't keep my hands to myself." He raked his fingers over his own hair, which was too short to hold on to. "I never want to hurt you."

"You haven't. So you needn't say more."

"No, I must. I promised to protect you, but when you're this close, I can't stop reaching for—" His hand halted an inch from her hair. He jerked back.

She did too. Water splashed. She inhaled sharply and swiped at the wet spot on her skirt, keeping her gaze down and hidden from him. "It does no good to talk about these things."

"Silence makes it worse. What if I said nothing, and you caught a cold *or worse* from being outside with wet hair and no coat?"

Mam had seemed invincible until she wasn't. The misery of her last days clenched his chest like a vise. The doctor had called her affliction pneumonia, but Da had blamed Robyn's birth.

"I'll be fine." Oriole tossed the water from her bucket and bent to scoop up a pristine patch of snow. "I've done this before, you know."

She was right. But so was he. But the more he argued, the longer she remained outside, with silky wet hair he'd now touched. His fingers fidgeted for a second chance. He thrust his fists into his pockets and sealed his lips against being a distraction that would keep her with him any longer than necessary.

I want her to go inside her wagon. Yeah, to dry her hair and don her coat, then come back outside and talk with me.

He paced a short line to stop his feet from wandering

her way, while she took a blasted long time filling her bucket. Almost as if she wanted to linger and torment him.

The echoing yips of two coyotes made her bolt upright. She stood stiff and silent, scanning the darkness.

He swallowed the impulse to tell her not to worry. A pair of coyotes wouldn't harm her or her horse. They'd be after smaller prey. She'd know that. Her life in a musical troupe traveling from town to town had probably put her in a camp like this many times.

So why did she keep staring into the shadows like they might devour her?

She clutched her bucket in a white-knuckle grip. Her other hand pressed flat and hard against her stomach because...she didn't have her violin or her sisters' hands to hold. She'd never camped alone.

Her tough act was a smokescreen.

He moved to stand beside her. She didn't look at him, but her shoulders relaxed. Until a black and white blur tore out of the dark and dove into her wagon.

Oriole's bucket hit the ground as she jumped back. "What was that?"

He froze in surprise. He'd never seen her so startled. She now clutched both hands over her heart.

What had he missed? He braced himself to pull his pistol from under his coat. "Looked like a collie dog."

"He was fleeing the coyotes," she whispered.

No hint of their pale brown bodies showed in the dark. Wherever they were, they were keeping their distance. The blur that'd raced inside her wagon hadn't been large. A small dog was the perfect size of prey.

"He's lucky he found shelter in your wagon."

"They were hunting him." She shivered.

He whipped off his coat and slung it over her shoulders, all while cursing himself for not doing so sooner.

Her eyes flashed up at him. Rimmed in white, her irises held hardly any color. "I can't take your coat."

"You're borrowing it until you can retrieve your own."

"Thank you." She hugged the garment closer and strained to see inside her wagon.

Rather than dwell on how a man could be jealous of his own coat, he focused on his first time seeing the interior of the wagon Oriole had lived in for the past week.

On the left and right, the one break in the drawers and cubbyholes was a bench seat opposite a stove so tiny it could only heat one pot at a time. The rear wall had a small window with red and yellow curtains above two bunks. One on the floor. The other halfway up the wall. Both heaped with blankets, even more colorful than the curtains.

"He's on the bottom bunk." Oriole's verdict vibrated with dismay.

Nothing on the bed moved or made a sound. In the hush, his and Oriole's footsteps crunched the snow as they crept in for a closer look.

"How can you tell?"

"The blankets weren't *that* messy when I left." Her miffed tone made him grin.

He could handle her being cranky, but not scared. "Looks like you've got a new roommate."

"This isn't funny."

"Not even a bit?"

"I want my wagon back."

"You could always take the top bunk and leave him the bottom."

Her sigh was beyond weary. "I couldn't sleep with him that close."

"Do you want me to get him out?"

She stared at her bed for a stretch as long as it was hopeful. At least on his part.

"No, I'll do it. I'll..." She trailed off as if at a loss for what she would do.

Helping her with the dog could be a step toward proving his value. If he wasn't obvious about it. Best to make whatever came next sound as if she were doing him a favor.

He strove to keep his tone casual. The exact opposite of how he felt. "It's been a long day."

"It surely has."

"My family had a collie when I was young. Mind if I went in your wagon and took a look at him before heading to my tent?"

"You *like* dogs?"

Didn't most people? A silly question he was glad he hadn't voiced aloud because she obviously did not. He replaced his impulse to ask why with a shrug and a simple, "Yeah."

"Be careful he doesn't—" She stopped as abruptly as she'd started.

"Doesn't what?"

Her shrug mirrored his from a moment ago. "Just be careful."

He expected her to retreat as he climbed in. She didn't. She stayed as close to the wagon as one could without going inside.

With his gaze locked on the bottom bunk, he moved slowly, murmuring a litany of words he used with skittish horses, aiming to reassure both Oriole and the dog. The wagon's low ceiling forced him to bend his back. Hopefully, that would help him appear less threatening.

When the mutt finally peeked above the blankets to see

who approached, Heddwyn winced with commiseration. The dog whimpered and went back to hiding.

"What's wrong?" Oriole's whisper drew him to her.

He dropped to one knee in the wagon's doorway, wondering how to deliver the news. "We have a problem."

"You mean beyond a stray taking over my wagon?" Her tone was perturbed, and rightfully so.

"He bumped into a porcupine."

The fall of her dark lashes concealed her eyes as she stared past him. "How many quills are in him?"

"A dozen or so. We need to remove them before his nose swells any more. Does your rig have a toolbox?"

"Bottom drawer on your right."

Everything needed to maintain a wagon was there. Either the drawer came fully stocked, or Oriole had added to it. After witnessing her travel savvy, he'd put his money on the latter.

He chose a pair of pliers. "We can use these to grip the quills and pull them."

"You've done this before?" Her face remained downcast, but her voice sounded hopeful.

"I helped my mam when I was a boy."

"Is *mam* Welsh for mother?"

"Yes, mine was a schoolteacher before she married. Every day was an education and an adventure. She made learning fun."

"So, that's how you taught Robyn so well. Wren always wondered."

"Wouldn't say we did anything well. We mucked up a lot, but Mam always said as long as we tried, she'd be proud. She told me how to remove the quills while she held our dog still." He worked the handles of the pliers, making sure they opened and closed easily. "She wanted me to show my brothers later if need be."

"It's a two-person job." Oriole's conclusion sounded like the end of the world.

Mam had never rushed them into doing anything they feared. He didn't have time to ease Oriole into tackling what had to be done. She needed to get back inside her wagon and out of the cold. "I'll take him to my tent and pull the quills there."

"What if he runs off before you can? Will the quills fall out? Eventually?"

He wouldn't lie to her, but he could soften the truth. "I don't know, but you don't have to worry because I'll hold him tight."

"How can you do that and remove quills?"

"Necessity is the mother of invention. I could make a collar or—"

"Stop saying *I*." When she climbed into the wagon, he jumped to his feet and almost hit his head on the ceiling. She closed the door behind her. "The dog stays here until *we*'re finished."

"I hope we're never finished." The tiny interior gave no room to retreat or hide from words that were true and false at the same time. "I mean..." He frowned at the pincers in his hand. "This isn't a good idea."

Her toe tapped the floorboards. "What isn't?"

"You being so close. *To the dog*. He's scared and hurting. He might—" He clenched his teeth. His compulsion to protect her was probably frightening her more.

She released a slow breath. "I've been bitten by dogs before."

"You have?" His gaze leapt to her while hers remained fixed on the floor between them. "When? In Cheyenne?"

Why hadn't he ignored her rule to only be together in dark alleys? He should've escorted her everywhere instead of following her at a distance to ensure she always returned safely to her sisters.

"It was before we met. Even before Lark and Wren. But none of that matters now."

"The past matters." If it didn't, why did it invade his thoughts more often than not?

A few days ago, he'd quizzed Lark about her life before her songbird troupe days. She'd patiently told him about the French missionaries, the Métis, and the Cree in the Qu'Appelle Valley. Then she'd looked him straight in the eye and said he'd have to ask Oriole if he wanted to know more about *Oriole's life*, especially before the orphanage. All Lark knew was that Oriole's mother was Cree and her father was an Irishman she'd never seen. Lark and Wren shared that history, but no family. The first time they'd met was at the orphanage after their mothers died.

Losing a mother or father was a world-shattering event, but at least he'd known both of his parents. Oriole, Lark, and Wren had not. And Robyn had three bumbling brothers who'd tried to do what a father and mother might. His sister knew everything about her past because they'd told her hundreds of stories about the good times and the bad.

What would it have been like to suddenly lose both your mother and the world you'd shared?

"I'm sorry your mother died."

"I'm glad she left."

Surprise robbed him of a reply. Leaving wasn't the same as dying. Or was it? His dad had chosen to leave his children by ending his life.

Oriole's gaze darted everywhere but toward him. "I shouldn't have said that. And you shouldn't have questioned

Lark. You're the nosiest person I've ever met." She stopped squirming only when her gaze fixed on three violins hanging above the bench seat.

He'd been so focused on Oriole and the dog he hadn't noticed them. Why did she have them and not her own? Now wasn't the time to question her motives. Not when he hadn't stated his own.

"Do you ever wonder why *I do* what I do?"

"All the time," she muttered.

Her answer, however gruff, encouraged him. She hadn't said no.

"I asked Lark because if I continue knowing nothing about you, I'll keep saying the wrong words. And you're the person I want to talk to the most."

It was her turn to gape at him. The glow of the lantern made the amber in her eyes glitter like gold. "That can't be true."

"It is!"

Only when she flinched did he realize he'd shouted. But she didn't look away. The heat in her direct appraisal made him jittery with questions. Was she still determined to shut him out? Or did she want answers as well?

The dog's whimper broke their standoff. They needed to focus on helping him first.

"I'll hold him while you pull the quills." He held out the pincers for her to take.

Oriole hung on to the coat he'd given her. "What if I'd rather hold him?"

"Then we're heading for another quarrel 'cause I refuse to let another dog bite you. Only by holding him myself can I ensure that." He rubbed the crick in his neck from stooping too long under the wagon's low ceiling. "Look, I know you could handle either task, but I need you to do one."

"How do you *know*? You just admitted you know nothing about me."

"You're right. I'm guessing you've survived a helluva lot tougher situations than this."

She shrugged. "I had Lark and Wren's help."

"And now you have mine. I can"—when she frowned, he rephrased promptly—"*we* can use my coat to cover him except for his nose. That way he won't see the pincers coming." And Oriole wouldn't have to look the dog in the eye. That had been the hardest part when he'd helped Mam.

She handed him his coat. Then she took the pliers and clutched them in the same white-knuckled grip she'd used earlier on her water bucket. "I'm ready."

When he turned in search of the dog, he found him pressed against the back wall, looking desperate to escape the wagon and them.

Oriole gasped. "He's barely half grown." She grabbed his sleeve and tugged him down until they both knelt. "If we make ourselves smaller, he might not be so scared."

The swiftness of her actions surprised him until he remembered that she, like him, had been looking out for a little sister most of her life. Had his size ever frightened Oriole? She wasn't tiny like Wren, but she wasn't as tall as Lark either.

He began his litany of soft words again.

With Oriole as his partner, the extractions went quickly. Her hands didn't shake as she pulled the quills, but her eyes glistened like the mist. When she finished, he gathered their patient in his arms and stood. The dog whined but didn't struggle.

"Easy there, little fella. I'm just taking you to my tent." He didn't look at Oriole. He'd only delay leaving if he did.

Outside, her horse's snorting and stomping mingled with an undertone of growling.

"My mare." Oriole yanked a rifle from a box under the bench seat. By the time he set down the dog, she was out the door.

He drew his own pistol and tore after her. "Oriole, wait!"

She froze at the bottom of the steps with her rifle aimed at his tent. The canvas was rocking every which way. He pointed his pistol skyward. His gunshot reverberated in his ears and into the night.

Two coyotes leapt out of his tent and ran off without a sound. Most likely because their mouths were full.

"Hungry little devils."

Oriole lowered her rifle. "This is a disaster."

He sought to lighten her mood with a joke. "Only if they've taken my jerky and left the biscuits."

When Oriole trudged away from him and toward her mare, he went to inspect the damage to his home for the duration of his travels. The missing food wasn't the worst of it. He'd tied the tent flap so well that the coyotes had to chew their way inside.

"Is your tent ruined?" Oriole didn't look at him as she petted her horse.

"It's seen better days." It was also ripped beyond anything he could repair. "I'll ask at the farms we visit tomorrow for something I can buy as a patch." Or as a replacement. "How's your mare?"

"Fine." When she didn't say more, he made a beeline for her.

Once again, she was without a coat. She leaned against

her horse, probably gaining as much comfort as she sought to give.

"The coyotes got what they wanted. They won't be back." At least not tonight. He holstered his gun to show her he wasn't worried, so she shouldn't be either.

She held her rifle awkwardly, like she hadn't handled one often. She hadn't hesitated to grab it, though.

"I'm not worried." Despite her firm reply, her shoulders drooped. Fatigue gnawed at her I-can-handle-it-all act, which he realized wasn't so much an act but a way of life.

She raised her chin and headed for his tent.

He kept his distance as he followed her. "Oriole, have you ever been...scared of me?"

"No. Of course not. Why would you ask me that?" She glared at his tent. "We need to gather whatever's worth salvaging."

"I'm asking 'cause a moment ago you worried how us being bigger than the dog would make him feel."

"Because he's young. Everyone's scared when they're young." She planted her free hand on her hip. "Where are you going to sleep?"

"Right here." He gestured to his tent. Some tent was better than none.

"You mean in the tent that's missing one end because of me?"

"That's not your fault."

"If I had handled the dog on my own—"

"Pulling quills is a two-person job," he reminded her.

"But if you'd stayed outside, those coyotes wouldn't have wrecked your tent. We both know it's now useless in this weather." She spun to face him with a challenge in her eyes. "It's a good thing you like dogs."

He ran his hands over his hair to stop himself from reaching for her. "Why?"

"You'll be sharing the bottom bunk with him."

He shook his head. *You need rest more than I need comfort.* "You said you couldn't sleep with a dog in your wagon."

"That's your greatest worry? If I get sleep?" Before he could answer, she added, "For better or worse, we're spending the night together."

"Don't marriage vows begin that way?" He froze in disbelief. Had he really said that aloud?

A slight widening of Oriole's eyes was her only reaction. "You can be as silver-tongued as the Roma."

The thought of her being surrounded by men endowed with a legendary gift of gab made his soul rage with jealousy.

"They," Oriole added, "are another example of why one should avoid talking."

"That's hard to believe." He gestured to her rig. "Whatever was said earned you one of their wagons."

"They'd told me Wren left their camp just before my arrival. I was that close." She exhaled wearily. "I needed the wagon to keep going. I gave them the money I had, but they wanted more."

When she went silent, he forced himself to speak casually and not like her answer was essential to his peace of mind. "So they asked for…?"

"They didn't ask. They made me vow to do a task for them and then…" She heaved another sigh as she circled his tent, looking for something.

He gritted his teeth and counted to five before saying, "And then?"

"Their headman added a pledge to consider a union with them."

His world lurched, and his words exploded. "You mean marriage?"

"I mean music." Her growl gave him hope. She stopped circling his tent and plucked his packsack from the ruins. When she threw it at him with a vigor that stung, his spirits soared.

Even while exhausted, Oriole never gave up. Or gave in. The depths of her resourcefulness seemed endless. The Roma may've been demanding, but Oriole was unconquerable.

"They desire a replacement for the musicians they recently lost. The wagon belonged to their best performers and teachers. After the elders died, the daughter, Alafair, disappeared without a trace. The sudden loss of three souls was unsettling. They were discussing burning everything owned by the deceased in a ceremony to destroy all material ties to the dead."

He'd heard a similar tale from his da. "They fear their relatives' spirits won't rest."

"It's an old superstition." She crouched to add his gear to the sack he held.

He did the same. "And an expensive one."

"But not, I suspect, a common practice for this particular group. They argued a lot. Whatever the case, my arrival—so soon after the deaths and disappearance—was deemed a sign."

He nodded. "You were carrying your violin back then. And now you have the gypsies' violins."

"The three on the wall are replacements. I'm merely a facilitator who cleanses any link between the living and the dead. I gave the instruments to Mrs. Fitzgerald in exchange for new ones. Or at least, new to the Roma." Still holding her rifle, she struggled to lift the remnants of his tent and shake off the snow.

He slung his sack over his shoulder and grabbed the other end. Their teamwork soon had the torn canvas folded as neatly as it could be. They walked side-by-side back to the wagon.

"You promised the gypsies you'd come back."

"I think they prefer the name Roma." Her gentle scold had him nodding again.

He wasn't his da, and this wasn't the old country. He wanted to do better. He needed to use the right words. "How soon must you return?"

"As soon as I can. They want their clan to continue being musical. I want to find Wren. I hoped to have accomplished that already. Then I'd only see the Roma once more."

"They'll be hoping for more than a few hours of your time." He shared that desire keenly.

"They get an entire night."

"What?" He slammed to a halt, remembering her previous words. She'd vowed to consider a union with the Roma. "What happens *exactly* when you see them?"

She stared at her wagon; her profile hard and determined.

"Oriole—"

"My vow includes talking with them *honestly*." Her voice rose on the last word as if it were impossible. "And I must also teach music to anyone who asks. In the morning, I'm free to leave. Or not." She threw her hands in the air before crossing her arms over her chest like a barricade. "They believe I'll choose to stay. Eventually. Every time we meet, I must repeat the process."

"Until you give back the wagon?" He held his breath, willing that to be the case.

"Until we never cross paths again. After I return Wren to Lark's care, I'm heading west. I won't stop until I reach the ocean."

Her declaration rocked him on his heels. "What about settling in Songbird Junction?"

"That's Lark's home." She climbed the steps of the home he'd always assumed was temporary.

"But Grandpa Gus named the junction not just for Lark but for you and Wren."

"He did that for Lark. He doesn't *know me*." She paused in the doorway to stare at the bottom bunk—and presumably the dog once again hiding there. "Did *you know* there are towns in California called Ventura and Los Angeles? Even the fairytale of angelic good fortune sounds better than my same old song."

She still believed he didn't know her. But with each word, she changed that. Oriole longed for change. The simple solitude of Songbird Junction would provide that, but not a lot more. He preferred the bustle of Denver. Maybe she did too.

"You could stay with Mrs. Fitzgerald." *And then I'd see you every day.* That was the change he craved.

Her spine stiffened. "She deserves a real granddaughter. I'm cursed to wander. It's in my blood."

"Or maybe moving is part of a past you were never free to shape. Now you are. If you really wanted, you could stay with your sisters." *And me as well.*

"They're...better off without me." The waver in her voice betrayed her tough act again. "All I do is lie. When I break my vow with the Roma—and I will, I'll be doubly cursed."

"But you just told me you did what they wanted and were going back to them. Was that a lie?"

"No." She finally turned to face him. "And I don't understand why I'm telling you the truth."

"Maybe because you don't know yourself so well either."

"I know that my vow includes honesty while I'm in the Romani camp."

He climbed the stairs, only halting when their eyes were level. "I have a solution."

She held her ground and his gaze. "It won't work."

"It already has." He kept his voice calm, but his heart raced beyond his control. "For the first time, you've been honest with me."

The light in her irises flickered like a candle caught in a cross breeze. "For barely an hour."

He forced himself to stay still, to not even blink as he said, "What if honesty is a learned behavior? You should practice on me."

CHAPTER 6

For what felt like the hundredth time, Oriole's gaze went to Heddwyn walking alongside her wagon. She resisted her ongoing urge to suggest he ride with her. If she gave in, she'd be giving up on making him go home. How many miles would it take before he grew weary and left her?

His stride was as tireless as his arm, throwing a stick for the dog to retrieve for a lot of praise and petting. The dog wiggled with delight. He'd been completely charmed into forgetting about porcupines, coyotes, and baths.

Heddwyn had insisted both he and the dog needed a scrub before staying in her rig. He'd also insisted she climb under the covers of her bunk while he did the work. Not only melting snow for washing, but for her horse to drink. During the chaos, she'd forgotten that task.

She couldn't forget that Ulysses would hurt anyone who helped her.

For his own good, Heddwyn had to go home. His idea of practicing anything with her was a temptation, not a necessity. She might find Wren and the Roma today. If she did, she'd never see Heddwyn again. She'd been lucky to have an entire night with him, even if she'd seen little of him.

He'd heated the bathwater inside her wagon, but he'd washed himself and the dog outside. She'd never pegged him as the modest type. But his restlessness remained unchanged. He'd tossed and turned on a bed within arm's reach below hers.

The only time Heddwyn had remained still was when she'd persuaded him to stop talking while they'd kissed. What would he have done if they'd...done more than kiss? Anything done with passion was a good way to release tension. Heddwyn drove wagons like their wheels were on fire. She played the violin like her fingers were. Common activities for both of them.

Her thoughts centered on one very heated but uncommon—at least to her—activity she and Heddwyn might do together in order to release both of their rest-lessness.

"It wouldn't be much different from brushing your horse." Heddwyn's proclamation left her sputtering.

"It—it wouldn't?" *It* couldn't be what she'd been ponder-ing. Her amorous daydream had landed her in a conversa-tion she probably should be ignoring.

He gestured to the dog running back to him with the stick. "Petting him. You could try when we make camp."

The tumult in her head and heart turned to confusion. "Why would I want to do that?"

"Because you keep looking at him."

Not at him. *At you making him happy.* While all she'd done was hope to return the dog as quickly as possible. But what if he hadn't come from a good home? What if he, like her, was a runaway?

That possibility made her squirm on her wagon seat

while Heddwyn went unnaturally still. He paid no attention to the dog trotting by his side. Instead, he scowled at the road as if spying something distasteful.

Nothing appeared out of the ordinary. Except for Heddwyn, who kept finding ways to surprise her.

"After I left Mrs. Fitzgerald's shop, how did you find me?"

"I followed your wheels."

"Along the alley, yes. You couldn't have seen them in the chaos of tracks on the thoroughfare."

He shrugged. "I gambled on you going straight after you turned at the crossroads."

"You guessed there as well?"

"Your rear wheels curved slightly and pointed the way." A fleeting smile quirked his lips. "You did a fine job of waiting till the last moment to turn and hide all but a shadow of your intent."

Only a life working with wagons would've made anyone notice a detail so faint. When she studied him more closely, she noticed something as well. He wasn't staring at the road, but at a ramshackle house near it.

"You know who lives there?" she asked.

"Only by reputation. I hope the dog isn't theirs."

"Why?"

"He deserves better. Everyone does. Last year, Robyn brought them a package they couldn't collect themselves or pay anyone to deliver. Instead of thanking her, they berated her."

She bristled in defense of his sister. "For what?"

"Doing a man's job, wearing trousers, having the devil's coloring, and on and on." He stroked her mare's head as he crossed in front of her to reach the side of the road closest to the house. He'd put himself between Oriole and whatever lay ahead.

The maneuver was as familiar as it was surprising. She and Lark always positioned themselves to protect Wren. They'd never had someone do it for them. "What's...the devil's coloring?"

"According to the husband and wife in this house, Judas had red hair."

The missionaries had spoken of the man's betrayal, but not his hair. And she'd been too busy disliking her eye color to consider anyone's hair.

"Griff was keen to pay them a visit and show them what the devil really looked like." Heddwyn's gruff tone made her suspect he'd wanted to do the same.

An urge to lighten his mood made her ask, "And your big brother said...?"

Heddwyn's much too brief rumble of laughter left her craving more. "Bryn convinced us to invest our time with those who valued actions and not appearances. Or was it deeds and not differences?" He shrugged. "Whatever it was, we steered clear of this house."

She'd never given much thought to his family being different. Not even after Lark told her that Robyn had tried to transform herself this Christmas, but ended up the same as ever. Much to the relief of her brothers and Max. Two years ago in Cheyenne, Robyn had always seemed remarkably confident in, and comfortable with, who she was. And Wren had always wanted to learn why, so she could be the same.

Oriole couldn't wait to see Wren's expression when she learned how the Llewellyn brothers had gained their flair for teaching from their schoolteacher mother, who'd made learning an adventure.

But first, she had to find Wren.

"Whatever this couple says, I must ask if they've seen Wren." She halted her wagon by a footpath winding its way through a circle of stumps and logs around the house. Cutting trees that weren't then used for buildings or firewood made the land appear abused.

"I imagine," Heddwyn said with a sigh, "they'll have plenty to say about a woman traveling with a man who isn't a relative."

She jumped down from her wagon to stand beside him. "That's one reason Ulysses lied about being my uncle."

"If it helps, feel free to tell them we're married." Heddwyn didn't blanch after his declaration. Not like last night, when he'd compared her words to marriage vows.

"What happened to me practicing to be honest with you?"

He shrugged. "I honestly believe any lie that protects you is a necessity."

The door to the house opened to reveal a youthful woman with an eager expression.

After Heddwyn's weighty description, she'd expected someone older and a lot grimmer. She raised her voice to call out to her. "Sorry for the intrusion, but I'm looking for my sister."

The woman nodded as she held the door wide. "Come in, and we'll talk."

"Well, that's a warmer welcome than I envisioned," Heddwyn muttered as he followed her along the footpath. "It's like she's a different person."

What if she was? When her footsteps halted, so did Heddwyn's. Had he suddenly wondered the same thing she had? Only the warmth of his body told her that she wasn't on her own. Heddwyn stood close behind her, while the home in front of her now appeared neglected to the point of abandoned.

The woman shivered and wrapped her arms around herself and her too-fancy-to-live-in-this-house dress. "Hurry up. It's too cold to stay outside."

Deputy Nash hadn't mentioned who'd sprung Ulysses from jail. Had a woman been involved?

This woman finally frowned. "What're you waitin' for?"

"Time to lie," Heddwyn whispered before saying loud enough for the woman to hear, "Wouldn't be right if we came in while you're alone, ma'am."

Oriole nodded. "It'd be different if your husband were home."

"I'm here." A man appeared at the woman's side. A thin man with red hair. The devil's coloring according to the people who *should be here.*

Disbelief then dismay held her speechless.

"And we insist that you join us inside...our home." The man grinned as he put his arm around his accomplice, and she did the same.

"What a relief," Heddwyn said as he moved to stand in front of her. As soon as he did, the gun he'd held hidden behind his back flowed like quicksilver to point at the couple. "Now there's no doubt. You both work for Tombstone."

The couple tensed as if preparing to release each other and reach for something else. She couldn't see a weapon, but chances were high they were armed in some way.

"Time to go, Oriole." Heddwyn's revolver didn't waver as he stared down its barrel at the pair glaring back at him.

When she retreated toward the road, he didn't follow her. She forced herself to keep going. The only way she could help him was to reach her wagon.

The man's voice cut through the silence like a knife. "What gave us away?"

"Your devilish hair," Heddwyn replied with a laugh.

"You're crazy," the woman hissed.

"Aren't we all?" Heddwyn's voice sounded resigned. "You let the great Ulysses T. Stone leave you here without a horse or proper winter clothing. You'll both freeze before you see a town again."

"You'll suffer a worse fate when your ladybird takes wing." The woman's glare jumped from Heddwyn to Oriole. "She's abandoning you here with us."

The air vanished from Oriole's lungs. Like a rabbit caught in a fox's stare, she couldn't move.

She doesn't know you. She can't see the truth. You're almost there. Keep going.

"Oriole's free to go wherever she wants. I won't stop her. I'm—" Heddwyn's words propelled her into action.

She leapt onto her wagon, reaching for the blanket behind her seat. "Stop saying I." She yanked her rifle from its hiding place and aimed it at the couple who dared to threaten Heddwyn. "*We* go together. Or not at all."

CHAPTER 7

*A*s soon as Heddwyn set his pistol by his boots and crawled into the bottom bunk of Oriole's wagon, the dog curled up by his side and didn't move. The collie's breathing flowed soft and steady. Lucky little fella to be able to doze off so quickly.

Even luckier me to get a second chance to sleep so close to Oriole.

Not that he expected to get much sleep. Same as last night, his gaze went to her bed above his, imagining her there. Arms and legs bare. The rest of her clad only in a shift.

Her dress and coat hung on a hook above her boots. His clothing was on the wall opposite. Like mirror images. However small, the wagon had been designed for two. Or more. For a couple with a child.

If he and Oriole had a daughter, they could share endless hours teaching her and watching her grow. She'd have Oriole's vibrant eyes and savvy strength. And he'd have everything he'd ever wanted, plus something he was only now learning he desired.

Turning his back to his dreams, he rolled onto his side and frowned at the rear wall.

Stop thinking about yourself. Don't think of Oriole either. No use thinking how she stood with you against today's challenges.

Like he'd always craved she would. Was she thinking about him too?

When his gaze went to her bunk, his head turned. Then his body. He flopped onto his back. The dog shifted to stay close to him and sighed in exasperation.

I know. I'm driving you crazy and me too. I need to move, to walk, to run.

Trying not to make any noise, he pushed back the covers and reached for his clothing.

"Where are you going?" Oriole's whisper in the air above him sent a shudder of yearning through every inch of his body—which was clad only in his long underwear.

He froze with his hand on the leg of his trousers, still hanging on the wall. "To...check on your horse."

"You heard something outside?" A flurry of wood creaking and blankets rustling erupted on the top bunk.

He donned his trousers as fast as he could. Only when they covered his lower half and, hopefully, his body's reaction to Oriole, did he dare to glance up.

Oriole leaned over the edge of her bunk, staring directly down into his gaze. Her breathless tone caressed him as she asked, "Is anything wrong?"

"No. Everything's wonderful." From his seat on his mattress, he had the best view in the world. "I was only contemplating going outside to stretch my legs."

Her smile blinded him. "You must have to fold up like an accordion to fit on your bunk. Accordions are my favorite next to my—" When she stopped, his thoughts easily formed the word she hadn't said.

Violin.

"You've every right to miss it."

"But I don't. At least not like I did before."

"Before what?"

She rolled back onto her bed and disappeared from his sight. "Before a few days ago."

That equaled the time they'd been on the road together. Ignoring the thrill making his blood race, he moved to sit on the bench where he could see Oriole's profile. She scowled at the ceiling. She was never comfortable when she disclosed a truth.

Say something smart. Something to keep her talking to you. He scanned the wagon for inspiration. His gaze stopped when it reached the three violins on the wall above him.

Why hadn't she kept her own? Dare he ask? She hadn't even wanted to say the word violin.

"How is it," Oriole asked, "that your mam taught you so many things but not...?" When she paused, he glanced her way. The return of her smile delighted him as much as her voice as she completed her question. "Not how to cook?"

She was teasing him. When he laughed, she did as well.

He'd done a dismal job of making their evening meal, but Oriole hadn't complained. She'd simply drunk a lot of water to wash it down. Their continuing closeness made him sigh like a man savoring his favorite dish.

"Mam tried." He sighed again. This time, with regret. "One can't succeed at everything."

"That's what I said."

"Really? When?"

"When I couldn't do everything to hide my departure from Denver. Still, I kept trying. Didn't your mam say that as well? *As long as you kept trying, she'd be happy.*"

The flow of Oriole words along with the good memories

of his mother relaxed him like he'd run a mile. He closed his eyes as he leaned back against the wall. "You're right. I won't give up on learning to cook." He snorted. "I don't want to choke on a stone-hard biscuit one day."

"I want to learn how to handle my rifle better."

"From what I've seen, you're doing fine."

She'd made sure they'd both survived the pair impersonating the farmers. All without a scratch. He should have questioned why the homestead appeared derelict to the point of abandoned, but whenever Oriole was near, thinking about anything other than her became darned difficult.

"Anyone can pull a trigger," she said.

His thoughts went to his father. "Yes, they can."

"I want to do better at everything."

He wanted the same.

Oriole's bunk rustled and creaked with a renewed vigor. He opened his eyes and caught a glimpse of her bare legs as she descended. His gaze plummeted to the floor. When she settled there with a blanket around her, he deeply regretted not staying in bed with the dog. If he had, he'd once again be in her direct line of sight.

"Reach out your hand to him. Slowly, so he can see you coming. Pause halfway and give him a chance to come to you."

When she did, the dog wiggled closer to her. She did the same until the mutt tucked his head under her hand.

She inhaled with wonder. "He likes me."

The lump in his throat made it hard to speak. "What's not to like?" he said gruffly. "Rub him behind his ears. He'll like that a lot."

She edged closer to the dog and did as he suggested. "You know what I like?"

"What?" He waited with bated breath for her answer.

"Learning new things."

He chuckled. "So do I."

"If that's true, I could teach you how to cook. Probably not *well*, but at least *better*." Her teasing tone—along with the prospect of spending more time with her—warmed him like a perfect summer day.

"And I could tell you everything I know about rifles."

"And more about dogs?"

"Of course."

"What would you have done if—?" She stopped petting the dog.

"If...?" he prompted.

"If you didn't have a gun and several dogs decided to follow you?"

He went tense with foreboding. "How many is *several?*"

She shrugged. "Let's say four."

His heart skipped a beat. "Dogs aren't like coyotes. In a pack, they can turn unnaturally vicious." He shook his head, not wanting to contemplate that or why Oriole had asked him this specific question. "I couldn't suggest much beyond finding a hidey-hole they couldn't reach."

"Like our dog did." She went back to petting him. "Back then I was also barely half-grown."

Anger made his blood roar in his ears. This was no hypothetical question. A pack of dogs had followed her. No, not *followed*. They would've *chased* her.

"Where was your mother?" he demanded.

She raised an eyebrow. "You get testy over the oddest things. This was long ago, you know."

"What I *know* is that you haven't answered my question."

"She was gone. She left many times but always came back. Until one day..." She shrugged as if it didn't matter.

"Until she didn't. I went looking for her, and the dogs found me. Luckily, it was summer. It took a few days for them to stop circling the tree I hid in. And my search continued. Only when I met Wren and then Lark in the mission's orphanage did I stop looking."

"And you told everyone your mother was dead."

She nodded.

His wrath turned inward. "I'm sorry."

A frown wrinkled her brow. "What for?"

"I left you in Cheyenne without saying goodbye."

"You had to go. Brynmor was injured. Besides..." She shrugged again. This time as if the outcome were inevitable. "I didn't expect you to stay after we quarreled."

He bit back his growl. When Griff raged, hardly anyone realized he was angry with himself rather than those around him. He didn't want Oriole to think they were at odds again. "I've had bigger rows with Robyn, and she's always been the pussycat in our family."

"I hate arguments."

"I'm not fond of them myself."

"I always say the wrong things."

"Me too."

In a heartbeat, Oriole's voice went from regretful to amazed as she said, "He's fallen asleep."

He was the dog. The mutt had dozed off with his head on her lap.

"Lucky little fella. He'll appreciate sleeping with you more than me. My tossing and turning exasperated him. You can take the bottom bunk if you want."

Cradling the dog against her, she crawled into his bed. He stayed where he was, waiting for his body's reaction to calm.

"Heddwyn, can I ask you...something else?"

"Yes." *You can ask me anything, Oriole.*

"If you made your bed on the floor, you could stretch out. And I could see you and ask what to do if the dog wakes up."

She could question him just as easily if he were in the bunk above. He wasn't going to point that out. He'd seize any chance to be closer to her. He yanked the bedding from the top bunk onto the floor, then lay down.

"Oriole...?"

"Yes?" The smile in her voice bolstered his confidence to continue.

"I know I'm not the first man you kissed, but I'd like to be the one who shows you many more firsts."

"I'm not like my mother." Her voice had gone cold and flat.

"Of course you aren't."

"Then why do you think you weren't my first for everything?"

CHAPTER 8

"*O*riole." Heddwyn's whisper caressed her ear. "You need to listen to me."

About what? Him being her first kiss? Or why he'd gone silent for so long after she'd told him he was?

"You need to open your eyes."

She did. Heddwyn's broad-shouldered silhouette—a familiar sight that still made her heart race—crouched close by her bed. The soft light of dawn peeking through the curtains tinted his hair her favorite shade of sunrise.

Waking up like this every morning would be heaven. When had she fallen asleep? What had she missed hearing him say? And most importantly, was he finally going to kiss her again?

He held his finger to his lips. "We're not alone."

She bolted upright. Their dog whined and pressed closer to her side. Heddwyn didn't move. Outside the wagon, the snow crunched as if a horde of invaders surrounded them.

"What is that?" She kept her voice as low as she could as she strained to hear.

Heddwyn did the same while still managing to sound surprised and then relieved as he said, "Sheep."

Their baaing became a distinct sound. A lullaby that should've comforted, but instead stretched her nerves tighter.

"Who's with them?"

"No one that I've heard. No woof from a sheepdog either."

Her hand went to their dog. Hers and Heddwyn's. Safe with them. Had he once belonged to someone outside?

That was a possibility she now dreaded but still must face. Heddwyn was already fully clothed and ready to go.

"I need to get dressed."

"I'll wait for you." Heddwyn rose and stood by the door with his back to her, giving her what little privacy he could. His gallantry brought a lump to her throat.

Even though they'd met in a rowdy barroom theater and he'd now seen her in her shift, he never stopped treating her with respect. Except for the first kiss he'd stolen. After that shock, kissing him had been as natural as breathing. She hadn't needed to be taught anything. Had it been so different for him?

Now wasn't the time to dwell on everything that kept them apart. She focused on donning her dress, boots, and coat as fast as possible. Then she tucked the dog under the bedcovers and murmured a reassurance that all would be well. She hoped.

After she retrieved her rifle from its hiding spot below the bench, she joined Heddwyn.

When she did, he drew his pistol and asked, "Ready?"

"Yes." Despite her agreement, she couldn't stop frowning at the door. What if they found Ulysses or more of his hirelings on the other side?

"We'll protect each other's backs." Heddwyn's fingers skimmed her hair.

Her gaze shot up to meet his, blue and steadfast.

"Our chances are better when we're together." His voice was hoarse, but his words were swift.

She nodded.

He opened the door and didn't pause. He went straight down the steps and into the sheep. She stayed close to him, covering their backs while he watched their front.

The wooly creatures—some with impressive horns curled close against their heads—flowed around them like a fleecy river, while the land beyond remained still and silent.

Tethered nearby, her mare nickered a greeting or a request for breakfast before returning to her dozing. Her calm reassured Oriole until something ahead of Heddwyn crunched the snow with a heavier weight and a slower tempo.

They halted in the same stride.

When she glanced around him and across the backs of many more fluffy beasts, she found a donkey loaded with gear—beside a man bundled in so much wool clothing he blended in with his flock. From a wrinkled face framed by black brows and a graying beard, he squinted at them with a youthful curiosity. He looked good-natured and in need of glasses.

Looks can be deceiving. Maybe he wasn't traveling alone.

She scanned the sheep again. The only secure spot was her wagon, to one side of them. Heddwyn had wisely kept them next to it.

The shepherd waved them forward. "Come closer so I can see you."

Heddwyn didn't move and kept his voice low. "He sounds familiar. His sheep are as well. They're Merinos. I think they're from the farm where I got Bryn and Lark's orphaned lambs." He raised his voice to call out, "Is that you, Mr. Diaz?"

Surprise widened the man's eyes. "Mr. Llewellyn? What're you doing here?"

"Helping a friend."

Mr. Diaz squinted even harder at them. "You're a long way from your freight office."

"As you are from your homestead," Heddwyn replied. "Must be lonesome work wrangling a herd on your own."

"I'm not—" The furrows in the old man's brow deepened. "Is this your wagon now?"

"It's mine." When Oriole moved in front of Heddwyn, he turned so they once again faced opposite directions.

He was protecting her back so she could take the lead. His elbow nudged hers. "Ask him about Wren."

"We're searching for my sister. She's—"

"No."

The man's abrupt reply made her jaw drop. "No, what?"

"I haven't seen her."

"How do you know? I haven't told you who she is."

"Go back to your people." His lips formed a hard line. Any trace of friendly interest had vanished.

Who did he think she was? *I have no people.* They'd shunned her mother for being an easy woman. And her mother had blamed everyone but herself. Until Oriole found Lark and Wren, everyone had shunned her as well. Or they paid her the worst kind of attention.

Heddwyn remained unusually silent. He was letting her find her own way forward.

She squared her shoulders. "My sisters are my only family."

"I've seen no one."

"So you keep saying." As soon as she voiced that truth, she suspected another. "You're lying." But she didn't know why.

He raised his chin. "I've seen no one except your gypsy clan. You should rejoin them. They aren't far away."

"They aren't my clan, my people, my anything."

The shepherd raised one eyebrow in challenge. "Now who's lying?"

She ground her teeth as she grappled for the right reply. What would he say if she told him the truth? *Yes, I'm a liar, but I'm not lying to you right now.*

He nodded as if he saw everything clearly. "You have their wagon."

A forlorn yip echoed inside it. Had their argument distressed the dog? Or was there something more?

"Can't see anything," Heddwyn said in answer to her unspoken question. "At least not on this side of the wagon."

They moved as one back the way they'd come.

"Wait," the shepherd hollered. "We're not done."

A flurry of barking made them sprint for the wagon door. In their haste to deal with the sheep, they'd left it open.

A younger-by-several-decades version of the older man stood on the bottom rung of the stepladder leading up to the door. How had he gotten there so quickly without them seeing or hearing him? He'd probably used the space under the wagon. That was, now that she'd had more time to think, what she would've done.

When the young man saw them, he jumped to the ground and backed away from them. He also kept his arms raised and his palms facing forward as if having failed to subdue the dog, he might succeed with them.

When the elder said, *we're not done,* he hadn't meant

their talk. His *we* was this pair. The elder had been a distraction, while the younger tried to take their dog.

She bristled with anger. As did their previously timid pup. He stood tall in the doorway and kept barking until he saw her and Heddwyn. Then he wagged his tail and lay down.

"Why do you want him?" Oriole demanded.

The thief blinked in confusion. "Him?"

"The dog."

"Oh, no. Not him. We..." He trailed off as his gaze went from her to the dog—or more precisely, over him to the wagon's interior behind him.

She released a relieved breath. Right now, she'd rather part with her blankets and toolbox than the dog.

"You're Tino, Mr. Diaz's grandson." Heddwyn didn't sound pleased that he knew this intruder as well.

The young man's face blushed bright red. "Sorry, Mr. Llewellyn. We didn't know this was your wagon."

"It's not," Heddwyn snapped with a gruffness that rivaled his brother Griffin's. "So, I'm not the one you should be apologizing to."

"We're real sorry, ma'am." Even with his head bowed in contrition, Tino couldn't stop his gaze from returning to the wagon.

"Yes, we are." The elder Diaz pushed through the sheep to stand beside his grandson. Instead of following them, he'd forged his own path around the opposite side of the wagon. "We meant no harm."

And yet they'd done what they could to distract her and Heddwyn so they could get inside the wagon. "Did you know the Romani family who owned this wagon before me?"

When neither man answered, she looked to Heddwyn

for any insight. He scowled at the chagrined thieves like he wanted to shake the answers out of them. Questioning them hadn't helped so far. Maybe discussing the wagon would.

"I'm sorry to say that the owners of this wagon passed and their daughter disappeared."

Her news elicited no reaction. Had they already known? From where the shepherds now stood, they had a view of the wall with the three violins. Tino's gaze moved restlessly over that area. To the untrained eye, the instruments must look the same.

"The Roma fear a person's link to their possessions might make them rise from the dead and haunt the living. Selling the wagon was their solution. Part of our deal was my trading the violins and bringing back these new ones."

Tino's gaze dropped to the ground. "That's why none of them look right."

"Hush now," his grandfather admonished. "They may not be related, but she's admitted to having a pact with those gypsies. She's bound to them."

Fury snapped her spine straight. "Nobody owns me anymore."

Both shepherds gaped at her wide-eyed.

"Who did before?" Mr. Diaz asked.

"Why should I answer your question if you wouldn't answer mine?" No good came from talking, but right now no good was coming from not talking. Lying suddenly seemed a hundred times more exhausting than simply stating the truth.

"His name is Ulysses T. Stone. He made me and my sisters perform for his profit. If he finds Wren before I do—" She tried not to think of the horrible things he might do.

He'd choked Lark for disobedience. What would his punishment be for running away?

"I owe the Roma nothing beyond the return of these three violins."

"Zin worships music," Tino mumbled.

She forced herself not to react to his declaration, to the fact that he knew the Roma headman by name. "I only play the violin. My sister Lark excels at every instrument, and Wren is by far the best singer."

Tino's expression turned puzzled. "Zin didn't try to make you stay with them?"

"He asked. I said no, then we discussed the wagon." She left out the Roma's muttering about the last time Zin commanded something of a violinist with unfortunate results. Being a runaway made her suspect that violinist was the daughter who'd *vanished*, which more likely meant *left without permission*.

Seeing the Roma again wasn't wise, but even if she hadn't vowed to do so, she would have. She must talk to everyone if she wanted to find Wren.

"You won't be staying with anyone if you don't want to," Heddwyn growled. "I'll make sure of that."

But previously he'd told her she should stay with her sisters. When she eventually left, what would he say? And do?

It'd always been difficult to imagine her life without Lark and Wren. The same was happening with Heddwyn.

"If either of you needs help..." Tino looked to his grandfather.

The older man nodded. "Come to our farm."

Their shift from foe to friend made her want to dance with joy. Instead, she shook her head. "Thank you for your kind offer, but I cannot accept. Ulysses has promised to harm anyone who helps me."

Mr. Diaz's chin rose higher than it had a moment ago. "We give sanctuary to anyone who needs it."

Was that what had happened with the Romani daughter? Had Alafair run away, and these two men were hiding her at their farm? It was probably best if she didn't know. But she could give them what they'd come for.

She went inside her wagon and retrieved Alafair's violin from its hiding place in a special cupboard. The instrument's dark-brown varnish, combined with a youthful abundance of painted red roses, contrasted sharply with the more traditional golden brown of the three on the wall. The sudden widening of Tino's eyes told her that difference was important to him.

When she climbed down to stand by him again, his eyes shone with tears.

"You kept it," he whispered in awe. "Why?"

"In case I found Alafair or someone who could return this to her." She didn't have to ask if he could. She just held it out for him to take.

His grateful expression spoke louder than words. With trembling hands, he took the violin. "You're an angel."

His praise made her as restless as Heddwyn, who now stood unusually still beside her.

"No, I'm just someone who believes an instrument creates a bond with a person, both living and dead. I won't tell the Roma that I gave you Alafair's violin."

Mr. Diaz seized her hand. "You wanted *to tell me* something earlier. Tell me now. Tell me what your sister looks like."

After she did, he squeezed her fingers. "I'm sorry. I honestly haven't seen her."

"Me neither." Tino carefully wrapped Alafair's violin in his scarf. "But if we do, we'll send you a message."

Her heart leapt with joy. She'd persuaded them to help her. And sharing the truth had been the key. She was no longer alone in her quest to find Wren. When she turned to share her happiness with Heddwyn and found him smiling at her, she remembered she hadn't been alone for days.

He'd stood by her even when she tried to push him away. She leaned toward him.

Mr. Diaz's grasp on her hand stopped her from doing anything foolish, like throwing her arms around Heddwyn. "We might even arrange to bring your sister to you."

Tino paused stowing the violin in a pack on the donkey to ask, "Where do you call home?"

Anywhere Heddwyn is.

That truth made her dizzy. When she looked to him as her anchor, her chest squeezed tight. He may still be with her, but his gaze was now elsewhere. He scanned the horizon.

She mustn't forget that their time together would end as soon as Ulysses appeared or was recaptured. Either she must leave Heddwyn to protect him, or he'd leave her when she was no longer in danger. He'd go home. Making up for the time he'd spent away from his family and their work had to be his priority.

The Diaz shepherds waited for her answer.

Wren is your priority. She exhaled a slow breath to steady herself and her voice. "If you can deliver Wren to the Llewellyns' office in Denver or the new water stop called Songbird Junction, she'll be safe."

"You'd be safe there, too." Heddwyn started to pace. "How far is the Romani camp?"

"An hour's walk southwest of here." Mr. Diaz snared Heddwyn's sleeve and pulled him toward her.

When Heddwyn came face-to-face with her, he went still as a mountain.

The sun crested the horizon and brought his hair to a full blaze, making the blue in his eyes even brighter. He'd always been a bewildering contrast. Impulsive, but consistent. Nosy, but respectful. He was the brother who'd helped raise a sister and build a thriving business without growing up along the way.

Heddwyn may still be a boy at heart, but the rest of him was all man.

"If you keep working together, all will be well." Mr. Diaz set her palm in Heddwyn's. Then he stepped back and waved for his grandson to follow him. "Time we got out of your way."

She stared at her hand, now engulfed in Heddwyn's, and...couldn't think what to do or say next. They'd kissed many times and slept in the same room, but he'd never held her hand. If their past was such a jumbled mess, how could their future be straightforward?

Heddwyn bent his head at the same time she raised hers. Slowly. Bit by bit. His lips came closer. Tantalizingly close. Not close enough. She leaned in. So did he.

They kissed like it was the first time, like every touch and angle and taste was new. She savored every part. She wanted it to last forever.

A forlorn yip disrupted their harmony. They both sucked in a startled breath.

Heddwyn's mouth hovered a whisper above hers. They didn't have to move further apart. They shouldn't. They could—

Their dog barked. Once. Twice. He didn't stop. He craved attention, too.

Heddwyn groaned. "Hush, little fella. Talking's—" He

cleared his throat, but when he continued, the passion in his voice remained strong. "Overrated."

"So is moving," she grumbled.

"Yes, it is." At odds with his agreement, his fingers started stroking hers.

She shivered with delight. Certain movements now deserved a blue ribbon, in her opinion. "None of us can stay still forever."

"We could go straight south and avoid trouble for a while." His suggestion tempted her.

All of him did. But she couldn't ignore the truth. Whatever direction she went, there'd still be trouble. And her own safety wasn't what mattered most.

"The Roma may have news about Wren."

"Do you think she ran away from them?" Heddwyn's hold on her may have been encompassing, but it wasn't restricting. He touched her like she might bolt at any moment, and he was preparing to let go.

Completely different from any hand she'd ever held. Totally discombobulating. He made it darned hard to concentrate.

"What do you mean?" she asked.

"Being as quiet as Wren is, I can't imagine her talking her way out of staying with the Roma if they discovered her musical abilities."

For the first time in her life, she was glad she hadn't given the violin back to Wren. "The Roma mentioned that Wren said very little to them, and I said—" She squeezed her eyes shut against her foolishness. "I told them we were all performers. Me, Lark, *and Wren*. I've put her in danger."

"No, you haven't. They probably sensed Wren was gifted from the moment she arrived."

"If they did—" A tremor of dismay shot up her spine.

"They told me Wren had left without them knowing." That now sounded disturbingly similar to another vanishing. "What if, same as with their own violinist, they tried to make Wren stay with them?"

And why hadn't she suspected them of lying? What else had she missed?

Under the expert guidance of the Diaz shepherds, the flock was halfway across the meadow. The pair knew what they were doing. They also knew Alafair's location but had said they didn't know Wren's.

Had that been the truth?

"My da told tales of the Romanichal in Wales. Every story was unique, but my favorites were always the same. I liked the ones with the violin or the harp. The players were as talented as they were resourceful." He nodded with conviction. "Griff said Wren was tougher than anyone thought. I guess both of us have always admired musicians."

But they, unlike Zin and Ulysses, had never coveted the money or prestige that might be earned from someone like her or Wren.

Heddwyn sighed. "Same as everyone else, the Roma will make assumptions about us traveling together. You shouldn't have to deal with me barging into your life uninvited." His frown deepened, but his hold on her hand remained the same. Gentle and loose.

"Losing Wren was my fault." She tightened her grip on him.

He did the same. "No, it wasn't."

"I reached for Wren's violin first and not her hand. That's why I left the instrument with Mrs. Fitzgerald. I had to start making better choices."

"I don't think you've had much choice in anything."

Heddwyn held out his other hand. Halfway. Like he'd told her how to approach their dog.

This time, holding his hand was a choice.

She took it. His hands now covered both of hers, keeping her safe and blissfully content.

More than ever, she wanted to do the same for him. "If I show you how to make breakfast, will you teach me more about my rifle?"

He nodded. "I'll explain how to use my pistol, too. You might need both when we see the Roma—whether we're staying with them for the night or running away from them."

CHAPTER 9

*O*n the wagon seat between him and Oriole, their collie wagged his tail with a joy that matched Heddwyn's. Oriole had insisted that the three of them ride together. Now whenever she caught him looking at her, she just smiled. So he just kept looking.

From the crown of her head to the tips of her toes, there were many captivating sights. Being able to study her without being scolded made his spirits soar as high as the mountains.

When they crested the next rise, his mood plummeted as fast as the trail to the valley below.

A hodgepodge of tents, campfires, and wagons similar to Oriole's dotted the snow along a rippling winter creek. The Romani camp buzzed with work and play until someone glanced up, waved at them, and shouted a hello. Once again, his time alone with Oriole was over.

His gaze went left, right, over his shoulder. All directions he'd rather go than straight ahead. In a single bound, the dog leapt off the wagon and under the closest tree.

Oriole pulled the wagon to a halt. She sat frozen, staring at the spot where the mutt had disappeared.

When she finally spoke, her tone was ominous. "This is where we part ways."

No, it isn't. He fought his need to snatch the lines from her and turn the wagon around. Whatever direction they went didn't matter. They'd accomplished too much to be separated now.

She'd held his hand and talked with him. He'd waited instead of rushing her. And *then* they'd kissed. Recalling the slow perfection of those three monumental events made him instantly hard.

Entering the Romani camp like a stag in rut wasn't good, but—like their direction—how he appeared was irrelevant. With so many eyes watching, he didn't have a chance of hiding much from the Roma. That didn't matter. No one in this valley could make him leave Oriole.

Their dog's familiar whine deepened to an unusual rumble. The little fella's instinct may be to hide, but he now growled like he wanted to protect Oriole as much as Heddwyn did.

He leaned sideways in search of a glimpse of him. "Maybe I can coax him out."

"Then what?"

He ran his hands over his hair, his neck, and his jaw. "Hide him under your bedcovers again?"

"I won't cage him." Oriole's refusal was as firm as her seat on her wagon. "This is his choice."

He'd done his fair share of retreating from Oriole, but it'd never been his first choice. Any place with her was his heaven on earth.

"He's free to leave," she added. "I'm not. After I hand over the violins, I'll find out about Wren. I'm only interested in the truth now." She snapped the lines, urging her mare forward.

They began their descent toward the people who waited on the edge of the camp for them. No, not them. For Oriole. They hadn't expected him to be with her.

Tough luck. This is my choice. He'd do anything and everything to keep Oriole safe and help her find Wren.

"So long, little fella." Oriole's hushed goodbye snapped his gaze back to her.

"Little fella?"

"Isn't that what you called him earlier? Don't you like the name now?"

"I like it a lot." *Especially when you say it.* He hoped they rejoined Little Fella soon so he could hear her say the name again. But first, they must tackle the Roma. Together. "Who gets the violins?"

"Zin. He's the one talking to Keomi, the woman with the lively hands."

Lively was an understatement. The colorfully dressed woman's gestures punctured the air between her and the annoyingly sturdy-looking man, who said little and moved even less. Zin's stoic strength reminded him of Brynmor. Eventually, Bryn won every battle.

He couldn't let Zin win today.

At this distance, no words were decipherable, but by all appearances the pair ahead appeared at odds.

"Which one of them is the leader?"

"Zin is their headman. Keomi is..." Despite her pause, Oriole kept the wagon at a steady pace. "She's harder to describe. By trade, she's a weaver, herbalist, and fortune teller. This clan's best at all three, I was told. They aren't married—to each other or anyone."

"So the leadership is split. That may work to our advantage."

"Yes." Oriole's reply was grim. "I should've questioned them separately to see if they told different stories about Wren."

"You'll do that today." *I'll make sure of it.*

With each turn of their wheels, they drew closer to their *welcome* party. The Roma's voices rose and fell but remained an indecipherable mutter, muffled by the creak of the wagon and crunch of the snow beneath it.

Heddwyn kept his voice low and tried to relax, aiming for a nonchalant posture far from his genuine state. "Besides Wren, what did you discuss the last time you were here?"

"Zin had many questions. What songs I knew. Who'd taught me. How long I'd performed. Could I teach others?"

"He's a musician?" The headman's single-minded interest raised his hackles. Oriole was more than her music.

"He'd like to be."

"And Keomi?"

"She talked of fortunes. Making bad ones better. She asked if I knew where to find new violins so she could break the link to their departed owners. That led to our discussing the wagon. At first, Zin opposed the sale. When my exchanging the violins was added to the deal, he agreed."

He'd made sure Oriole would come back. Heddwyn bristled like a badger guarding a den he had no right to claim as his own. Neither did Zin. Whatever the man hoped would happen when Oriole returned was *not* happening.

"Did Keomi agree with Zin?"

"In our one moment alone, she revealed Zin's obsession with making his lineage musical. He craved not only the funds but the security that an admired talent might bring."

He sounded too much like Ulysses.

"Alafair had that talent and also enjoyed teaching, but she didn't want to wed any of the Roma. Her parents respected her wishes."

Their two parties were close now. He scarcely had time for one more question.

"And after they passed away?"

"Keomi said Zin spread a rumor that she'd foretold a distressing future. Alafair's ability to play music would vanish unless she married a leader strong enough to halt such a tragedy. Alafair requested a last night alone in her family's wagon. In the morning, the only thing that had vanished was her."

Like Oriole and her sisters, Alafair had run away. But she had to leave everything behind to make her disappearance match Zin's prediction. Now, her violin would be returned. Oriole had made a poor fortune better.

Had that been Keomi's hope? Might she be an ally?

The Roma had gone silent. They were too close for private conversations now. And whatever words came next weren't his to say. Same as he had with the Diaz shepherds, he sealed his lips and waited for Oriole to lead the way.

When she halted her wagon in front of the Roma, she got right to the point. "I have your new violins. Do you still welcome their arrival?"

Keomi bowed her head gracefully. "We thank you for fulfilling this part of our agreement." The fortune teller's throaty voice held a compelling depth.

She reminded him of the wise old bards from his father's stories, except she didn't appear much older than him or Zin. And she was a helluva lot easier to look at than that man.

Zin's expression remained as rigid as his posture. "You

are welcome in our camp, but this stranger is not. He will stay with your wagon while we—"

"I'm not leaving Oriole's side." Heddwyn bit back his growl and strove for a more courteous tone. "I've pledged to protect her."

Zin snorted like a bull ready to charge. "How do we know she doesn't require protecting from you?"

Oriole's reply came lightning fast. "Because I say so."

"We must hear more before we can be certain." When Keomi turned to Zin, her voice grew louder while remaining profoundly composed. No doubt she used this skill often to make her declarations carry weight with her entire clan. "Our headman will judge the stranger's character. To safeguard Oriole *and* our people, Zin must speak with this man alone."

"Oriole's free to go wherever she wants, but I'm not. I'm not leaving her."

"So you keep saying." Zin's steely gaze clashed with his. "Now, you will listen to what I say. I will bring my wagon here, and you and I will talk inside it. If Oriole wants you by her side, she will stay near her wagon and wait for you."

And while she waited, she could talk to Keomi without Zin present. Oriole needed that. He just had to say he'd leave her.

His mouth refused to utter those words. Instead, he said, "It's up to Oriole."

A lengthy silence followed before she delivered her verdict for their future. "Speak with Zin, and I will see you soon."

CHAPTER 10

*B*ut what if she never saw Heddwyn again?

The question unnerved her. It always had. Today, she finally knew why.

She could survive without him, but now merely surviving felt like fading to nothing. Heddwyn brought color to every moment. Despite the short distance to Zin's wagon, her spirits slumped as she watched Heddwyn march away from her.

He couldn't do anything slowly or halfheartedly. He paused only once—to gesture to the three violins Zin carried. The Romani leader frowned before nodding. When Heddwyn took one, they continued without the danger of dropping Zin's treasured instruments.

Heddwyn hadn't a vindictive bone in his body. He couldn't stop helping. He wasn't doing this just for Lark and Wren, as she'd first believed, but for her too.

She had a job to do as well.

Question Keomi. Alone and uninterrupted. Her resolve rallied as she faced that task. Only one woman lingered beside the fortune teller. Everyone else had returned to their previous pursuits.

She couldn't lose this opportunity.

She cleared her throat to snare Keomi's attention before asking, "Will you join me in my wagon? I need to speak privately with you about Wren."

Keomi motioned for her to lead the way. But when Oriole reached her wagon doorway, the fortune teller halted with her foot on the stepladder's bottom rung and her comrade close by her.

Oriole struggled to keep her frustration out of her voice. "Please come in and—"

Keomi raised her palm. "I must run an errand first. Wait here, and all will be as it should be." When she stepped back, the other woman moved forward to block Oriole's way.

She tried to push past her. "Wait. Where are you going?"

"Be silent," the woman hissed as she shoved Oriole inside her wagon. "If you want Keomi to answer any of your questions, you'll hold your tongue till she returns."

"Make sure she doesn't follow me." Keomi's order was the last thing Oriole heard before the door slammed in her face.

The walls of her once-comfortingly snug wagon pressed in on her like a cage.

She bolted for the window above the top bunk. When she pressed her face against the glass, she glimpsed Keomi's blurred but colorfully clad form hurrying into the camp.

Where was she going? And why was it important for Oriole to stay behind?

She had to follow Keomi. And fast.

She retrieved Heddwyn's pistol from her rifle box. Thank heavens he'd shown her how to handle both weapons and agreed that entering the camp holding any weapon wouldn't set the right tone. The pistol's smaller size was her best option for maintaining that tone.

And if she couldn't? So be it. Discovering where Keomi had gone was now her priority.

She stowed the pistol in her coat pocket and pushed the bottom bunk's mattress sideways, just enough to reveal the trapdoor in the floor. Its hinges were as silent as Oriole had been ordered to be. Luckily, Keomi knew nothing about the part-time carpenter and full-time meddler who'd insisted on helping Oriole "spruce up" her wagon. Grandpa Gus hadn't batted an eyelash when she'd proposed this addition.

She jumped down to the ground beneath her wagon.

A droning sound made her freeze. Only a few feet away on the steps of her wagon, a woman's hemline swayed. To a tune. Of sorts. Her guard hummed with more self-satisfied gusto than rhythm or range.

Zin was right about at least one thing. This clan needed a music teacher.

She crawled away from her jailer's song and out from under the tail end of her wagon. Then she sprinted in the direction she'd last seen Keomi heading.

The web of wagons and tents—with ropes strung between as lines for laundry and tethers for horses and milk cows—slowed her search. Her legs ached and her lungs burned. She kept going. She couldn't stop. She had to find Keomi.

If she didn't, she might lose another chance to locate Wren. Every day she failed was another day Wren suffered alone. She couldn't let the Roma hoodwink her again.

A flash of color brought her skidding to a halt. If the fortune teller had shared Oriole's desire to look drab so

fewer people noticed her, she might've run right past Keomi
—and the man helping her saddle a horse.

Anger twisted her heart. Keomi had lied. She'd said
she'd come back.

No, she'd said, if Oriole *waited*, all would be as it should
be. She'd meant for herself. Not for Oriole. And more
importantly, not for Wren.

She yanked the pistol from her coat pocket. Keomi was
not leaving. She sprinted forward to make sure of that. Her
footsteps raced as fast as her heart.

The man helping Keomi leapt between Oriole and her
goal.

She halted with her gaze straight down the revolver
barrel she pointed at him. "Get out of my way. Or I'll shoot."

He didn't move. She couldn't miss a target so close. She'd
need more instruction from Heddwyn before missing any
vital organs. *Please step aside. Don't make me hurt you or—*

She forced the worst from her mind. Wren needed her to
remain focused.

"I'm only here for my sister. I just want to talk to Keomi."

The fortune teller left her guardian's shadow and
headed straight for Oriole. She didn't stop. Not even when
she nearly ran into the revolver.

Oriole jumped back and pointed her weapon skyward to
prevent a misfire.

The fortune teller seized her wrist and yanked her close
again. Oriole grabbed Keomi's arm to make sure they stayed
that way.

"You've more snarl than snap." Keomi's words hit like a
rattler's strike.

"I *have* what I came for," Oriole shot back. "You're not
going anywhere till I hear the truth about Wren."

Keomi snorted, then called softly to the man now too far

away to help her escape. "Stick to the plan. I'll keep her quiet while you go."

"I'll return." The man jumped onto his horse. "Fast as I can."

Dread made her screech. "Where is he—?"

"Shut up," Keomi growled as her free hand rose. Palm open wide. Winding up to slap Oriole.

Locked in her opponent's grasp, she couldn't retreat.

But she hadn't survived an institution full of wild children and disciplinary caretakers by standing still. When Keomi's hand swept down, she spun like a dancer. She used Keomi's own momentum to throw her off balance.

They fell together, both hitting the snow with a gasp of surprise. Or maybe a grunt of determination. They continued holding each other captive.

"You may've escaped your wagon, but you're still in my trap." Keomi's low but victorious laugh made Oriole shiver.

Hoofbeats departed at a fast clip. The rider was beyond her grasp. Wherever he was heading couldn't be good. She'd failed Wren. Completely. If she hadn't agreed to be parted from Heddwyn, he could've been here to help stop the man.

She had to get back to him, but she couldn't let go of Keomi. She tried to climb to her feet and bring the woman with her.

A crowd circled them. Like tall trees, they cast her in shadows. Rough hands seized her. They yanked the pistol from her hand and dragged her upright, breaking her hold on Keomi.

"Why are you attacking Keomi?" they demanded.

"I'm not." She forced herself to go still, to not bristle like a threat. "I was only trying to stop her from leaving."

"*Leaving?*" Keomi groaned as if gravely injured. "Why would I do that? This is my home."

"You—"

"I wanted to protect our headman. Our clan must do the same." Keomi's proclamation drowned her out like a bell calling warriors to arms. "This outsider assaulted me. Her man may be doing worse to Zin as we speak."

"He isn't." Outrage made her tone sharper than she'd intended. "You all heard Heddwyn. He didn't even want to go with Zin."

"She told him to go." Keomi's voice dropped to a whisper again. "Silence her—and we'll take him by surprise."

A hand clamped over her mouth. More hands pushed, pulled, and prodded her back the way she'd come. She had to escape them. She used every trick from her childhood survival book, plus the ones she'd learned under Ulysses' rule.

Her worst fears had come true. She hadn't found Wren. Instead, she'd lost her freedom and landed Heddwyn in terrible danger.

CHAPTER 11

*H*eddwyn struggled to sit still, to keep his gaze off Zin's wagon door and his mind off his wish that Oriole would open it. She'd tell him she'd found what she came for. They could leave together.

The world outside stayed hushed and hidden. The door remained closed.

Open the blasted thing yourself. Find out something—anything—about Wren.

He focused on Zin sitting on a stool between him and his goal. "Have you seen Wren since Oriole was last here?"

"No," Zin replied, like a troll guarding words and bridges.

"Have you heard anything new about her?"

"No."

The man's one-word answers irked Heddwyn as much as his continued stillness. They were as different as a firefly and the North Star.

He chose a question that required more than a single-word answer, like *no*. "Who's visited your camp since Oriole left?"

"Nobody."

He couldn't suppress his growl of frustration at Zin and himself. When had talking ever been so difficult? With Oriole, of course. But not today. Today they'd spoken effortlessly. Could that last?

His gaze shot to the door, then back to Zin.

The man's eyes narrowed like a hawk closing in on its prey. "How long have you known Oriole?"

His reply came easily. "Two years, three months, and nine days."

Zin's brows rose in surprise. "You followed her from Cheyenne to Denver?"

"No." He shook his head. He didn't want to discuss why he hadn't or couldn't. Why had he never gone back? Why hadn't he—?

He shook his head again. He needed to concentrate on helping Oriole *right now*. But if he, like Zin, gave only one-word answers, he wouldn't help anyone.

Oriole had stressed one word when she mentioned her previous talks with the Roma. *Honesty*. If they'd demanded that from her, they'd seek the same from him.

"After my parents passed, my siblings and I moved a lot. Always in search of work. Cheyenne was one of many places along the road." Until everything changed there. "We only recently found a way to settle in Denver."

"You were part of a musical troupe? Like Oriole and her sisters?"

He snorted in disbelief as he raised his hands for Zin to inspect. Meaty paws. Too big for the delicate strings of a violin. "Do I look like a musician?"

"More like a drudge."

It was his turn to be surprised. "*A what?*"

"A beast of burden. A field hand. A laborer. A—"

"I know what the word means."

"Then why did you ask?"

"I object to being labeled," he huffed.

"Welcome to my world." Zin folded his arms. "Tell me more about yours. Don't think. Just speak."

"I help run a post and freight company. That takes planning," he grumbled, then said on a sigh, "And patience." Two things he routinely struggled to master. "It's not all heavy lifting."

"But it's honest employment."

Honest. The word had finally entered their conversation. Was the headman starting to believe he might be honorable? Zin had already decided that Oriole was. Or had he? There was a difference between wanting someone and trusting them.

"A musical troupe can also be honest work," he replied.

"You defend them all?" Zin leaned toward him.

"Wren and Lark and Oriole."

Zin edged even closer. "But not their manager?"

"Absolutely not." He forced himself to sit straight and still, to not advance or retreat, not even an inch. "Have you met Ulysses Stone?"

"Heard talk of him."

Was he telling the truth? Even if he wasn't, he deserved a warning.

"In Cheyenne, my brother got too close to Oriole's sister, Lark. So, Ulysses tried to kill him. He only succeeded in blinding Bryn in one eye. That's when my family left Cheyenne. And I lost Oriole."

"Then Oriole came to you in Denver for transport?"

"She didn't *come to me* for anything. She didn't even know I was in Denver."

"But she's with you now."

"Because I insisted on helping her. And now..." He shrugged. "She's OK with it."

"Just OK?"

"We've discovered a way to work together."

"I see." Zin laced his fingers behind his head and lounged back on his stool, as far as he could, which wasn't far in the wagon's cramped interior. He appeared completely at ease, which was completely unfair.

"What exactly do you see?" Heddwyn asked from between gritted teeth.

"I wanted to help Oriole, but she was never *OK with it*. But you've known her for years, been traveling with her for days, and only left her side when she told you to go. And she did that reluctantly, which means..." Zin paused his summation like a Pinkerton agent at the end of a case. When he continued, his tone was resigned. "When will you ask her to marry you?"

Shock robbed him of a reply.

"It's a simple question." Zin's know-it-all expression irked him.

"No, it's not." Nothing about his relationship with Oriole was straightforward or permanent.

She planned to head as far west as she could. As soon as she could. He let his gaze roam the room so he wouldn't glare at the man or the door separating him from what little time he had left with Oriole.

Zin's wagon wasn't much bigger than Oriole's, but intricately carved and painted woodwork covered every surface. Nothing was simple here either. Compared to Oriole's wagon, Zin's was a palace.

"Who created this?"

Zin's smile was fleeting. "I did."

The man's carpentry and carving skills rivaled Max's

brother and grandfather. Why Zin was infatuated with music when he had this talent remained beyond Heddwyn. How had it come to this?

"Who taught you?"

Zin's hand dropped from behind his head to rest on his knees. "My uncle."

"It's a blessing having kinfolk who—"

"He died coming to America after outsiders forced us to leave our clan. They valued musicians, not tinkers." All traces of ease had left Zin's body. He once again folded his arms. Defensively.

Regret flooded Heddwyn. He'd discovered a truth, but only by dredging up a tragic memory. "I'm sorry."

"Now you're lying." Zin's glare pierced him. "You weren't there. You've no reason to be sorry."

"But I am. I'm sorry for every injustice that goes unchallenged. Including this." He gestured to Zin's craftsmanship. "This isn't a tinker's work. Not that there's anything wrong with that, but this isn't tinkering."

Zin's posture remained rigid. "For many people, it is."

Like him, Zin had been labeled. But unlike him, it resulted in Zin losing everything. He'd had to start from scratch. He'd survived and thrived. To a point. However elaborate, the wagon still lacked any hint of a woman's presence.

"You've built a new clan, but you still live alone."

Zin climbed to his feet. "We've talked enough. It's time to join the others." He gestured for Heddwyn to precede him out the door.

Had they truly *talked enough*? He forced himself not to spring to his feet and head straight for Oriole. Why had Zin chosen to end the conversation when faced with his own struggle to find the right partner? A musical one who, in Zin's experience, more people valued.

Value didn't lead to being treated well. Oriole and her sisters were proof of that.

He leaned back on his chair. "How long did Wren stay at your camp?"

"For one night. Same as Oriole." Zin tapped his fingers against his leg, looking as restless as Heddwyn felt.

He concentrated on not moving a muscle. "And she slept in the wagon you gave Oriole." Best to make the headman sound charitable. "Same as Oriole did after her."

"Wren lodged with Keomi."

"But if Oriole's wagon was empty, why didn't Wren stay in it?"

Zin's gaze locked on Heddwyn as he slowly reclaimed his seat. "What have you been told about that wagon?"

You worried it might be haunted. Saying that would've been rude but also inaccurate. Oriole had mentioned the group's reaction, not one person's, except when—

"Oriole said Keomi foretold a troubling fate for the wagon's original owner." He waited for Zin to fill in the rest, to repeat the rumor the man had spread. That Keomi had predicted Alafair's musical abilities would vanish unless she married a leader strong enough to halt such a tragedy.

"That's wrong!" Zin leapt to his feet.

The swiftness of the man's movement made Heddwyn jump as well. Both of their stools toppled and struck the floor with a bang. Two explosions separated by a second, like an echo of gunfire.

He strove to conceal his excitement. He was an inch away from getting another truth or a punch in the face. He matched Zin's stance, keeping his hands down but ready. "Are you saying your fortune teller can't see clearly?"

"Keomi hasn't *seen anything* in a month."

Shock made him reel.

"Someone's lied," Zin hissed.

Was it Zin or Keomi?

Zin's glare went to the door and stayed there. The headman wanted to leave as much as Heddwyn now.

He forced himself to stay put and ask, "When Wren left your camp, did she say anything?"

"I didn't see her go. Only Keomi did." Zin's tone went from furious to incredulous. "Keomi arranged everything. She made sure Wren stayed with her. Just the two of them."

"She's alone with Oriole right now." An invisible fist struck his gut. His hope that Keomi might be the one to help Oriole vanished along with his breath.

He bolted for the door, one step ahead of Zin. The portal burst open before he could reach it.

Two Romani men pushed through, single file, knives drawn.

He kicked the weapon from the first's hand before lining up a strike for the second. Scrapping with a pair of brothers had given him experience tackling two. Unfortunately, Zin and the men equaled three opponents.

A hand seized his shoulder and yanked him backward. "Stand aside," Zin roared as he shoved Heddwyn against a wall, then charged into the two intruders.

They fell flat on their backs in the snow while Zin maintained his footing and jumped down to circle them. Heddwyn followed him but kept his distance. He also kept his attention fixed on the men.

"You dare to enter my wagon brandishing weapons."

With bowed heads, the men scrambled away from their leader.

The one still holding a knife hurriedly pocketed it. "We had to check you were safe."

Zin froze. "Why wouldn't I be?"

Both of his men thrust their fingers at Heddwyn. "Because he's with you."

Unease coiled his stomach into a knot. "As ordered by Keomi."

"And your lady friend too," his accuser replied.

He spun in search of Oriole. Her wagon hadn't moved, but its door was wide open. No one stood near it. She was gone. He sensed it. Without a doubt. Like a nightmare that'd never fully retreated, a chasm of loss opened and threatened to swallow him whole.

"Where is she?" Why hadn't he stayed with her? Was she hurt or—? He couldn't bring himself to consider the worst. He steeled himself to do whatever was necessary to discover the truth.

"Speak!" Zin commanded his men.

"They're bringing the outsider back for your judgment."

Oriole was coming back to him. The revelation grounded him. His world stopped collapsing, but only for a moment. "Back from where?"

"The far end of the camp where she attacked Keomi. Last we saw, she was fighting like a demon to stop being brought back here to answer for what she's done."

CHAPTER 12

The instant Oriole saw Heddwyn sprinting toward her, she stopped battling the crowd dragging her toward him. She went limp with relief, then tense with astonishment. Heddwyn was unhurt. He was also angrier than she'd ever seen.

"Let go of her!" His roar had the desired effect.

Every hand released her immediately. But the throng didn't retreat. They circled Heddwyn as well. She braced for his realization that she'd not only abandoned her wagon and him, but she'd put him in grave danger.

"What's going on?" His glare scoured the crowd.

When he didn't even glance at her, her throat tightened unbearably. Same as when the Roma had silenced her with a hand over her mouth, she couldn't utter a word.

"Do you treat all of your guests so appallingly?" Heddwyn's scowl fixed on Keomi. "Why are you dragging Oriole around your camp?"

"That's her fault." Keomi raised her chin. "She should've stayed in her wagon."

"I've no idea how she got out," Oriole's guard mumbled.

"I do." Conviction rang in Heddwyn's voice. "You under-estimated her determination to find her sister." His gaze finally met hers. "Never hesitate to talk to me. I'm guessing Keomi wouldn't speak to you, so you did what you had to."

He still believed in her? The pressure on her throat vanished. "I followed her."

He nodded. "And then?"

"She joined a man saddling a horse." Her shoulders slumped. "I miscalculated. I thought she was leaving, so I grabbed her. But it was the man who rode off."

Heddwyn spun to face Zin. "Oriole and I are leaving."

"Not yet." Zin pushed past them to stand toe-to-toe with Keomi. "Not until you tell everyone—me, our entire clan, and our guests—what you've done."

Keomi answered without hesitating. "I made an agree-ment with her uncle."

A chill shot up Oriole's spine. "You've sent for Ulysses. Making Heddwyn talk with Zin was nothing but a distraction."

"I did not agree to this." Zin's tone went from furious to ominously neutral. "Who does?"

His clan shifted. Half stood behind him, the other behind Keomi, leaving Oriole and Heddwyn still trapped in the middle.

Zin didn't move except to cross his arms. "You've divided us."

Keomi matched his stance. "You did first."

Despite agreeing about their rift, the headman and fortune teller stood much too close. Oriole needed to drive a wedge between them and their clan. She had to pry open a crack just big enough for her and Heddwyn to slip out. And fast.

Ulysses or his thugs might arrive at any time.

"Whatever reward Ulysses offered you, he won't pay. He can't. He's out of money."

He'd lost his meal ticket when she and her sisters fled with the pitifully few coins he'd yet to squander from their labors. If she didn't leave this camp, she'd soon be paying for that theft. Even worse, she'd pull Heddwyn into that reckoning.

Keomi's glare didn't leave Zin. "This isn't about money."

He nodded. "I should've foreseen this."

"A true leader would have. Instead, you ignored me and our clan. You let your obsession with music blind you."

"I crave harmony and stability. A union between Alafair and me would've provided that." Zin huffed. "In time."

"Never," Keomi replied in her solemnly controlled fortune-teller tone. "Alafair loved an outsider but wouldn't abandon her parents for him. Only when they passed did she leave our clan because we've yet to become a real clan. And after Alafair departed, your attention shifted oh-so easily to the next available musician. *Why—?*" Her voice cracked before sinking to a whisper. "Why aren't my talents worth as much? Why aren't I enough for you?"

Astonishment made Oriole's jaw drop. Keomi had a craving as well. For Zin.

Was it love or obsession? Either way, furthering their divide wasn't the answer. Bringing them closer was. But how?

Her gaze went to Heddwyn. They'd started working well together. They'd acted like a team, but now...he didn't look her way. He stared at Zin.

"When will you ask Keomi to marry you?" Heddwyn's question hit like a bolt out of the blue, then felt completely right.

Before anyone could disagree, she said, "The best leaderships are often a pair."

"Who do not tear apart their clan." Zin threw his hands in the air. "We are too different."

"Not where it counts," Heddwyn replied.

"You both want your people to be strong." *And I only want to leave here with Heddwyn by my side.*

"Living for others is no longer enough." Keomi laid her hands on Zin's arms, still crossed in front of him—and separating him from her. "Do you remember how it was when we first met?"

The headman inhaled sharply, as if the memory had jolted him. "I do." He took her hands in his. "If we married, would you promise to bring harmony back to our clan?"

When Keomi shook her head, he bowed his to touch hers and still her.

"Forgive me," he whispered. "I should propose seeking harmony for us first and our clan next. Would you agree to that?"

"I would if..." Keomi's voice mirrored Zin's, low and earnest, as if it were just the two of them and not a conversation overheard by a circle of silent witnesses. "If you agreed not to place music above all else."

"I would if you agreed not to pursue outsiders' rewards unless we both...agreed." For the first time, Oriole saw Zin grin like a boy reclaiming an impish youth.

Keomi smiled back. "We've reached an accord that needs a seal."

Zin raised his head—and his voice for everyone to hear. "Keomi and I will marry by our campfire in a ceremony for all to attend."

"Oriole can't stay here." Heddwyn's posture remained rigid. "It's too dangerous for her and you."

What about for him? Ulysses would take one look at her standing beside Heddwyn and know she cared deeply for him. There'd be no hiding that truth from someone who'd watched her as long as Ulysses had.

"Where will you go?" Zin asked.

"To find my sister. And when I'm gone, Ulysses will follow me, and you'll be safe." Or at least she hoped they'd be. "You must defend your newfound harmony."

"What of yours?" Keomi asked.

Frustration made her stiffen. Why wouldn't they let her go? "Mine isn't here. It's out there." She gestured beyond the Roma.

"Are you certain?" Keomi's all-knowing tone made her bristle even more.

Heddwyn scanned the horizon, now dusky with twilight, and recited the phrase she'd heard members of his family say more than once. *"Only the daft, the desperate, or the devil travels the wilderness after dark."*

"And two unions double the peace." Keomi's gaze locked with hers. "You should wed your man as well."

"That's not possible!" Her outburst made her cringe.

Marriage was a trap and a dream. Something you fell into or never found. Either way, it led to heartbreak. She could only hope to stay with Heddwyn a little longer.

She had to leave and lead Ulysses far away from everyone. Not just the Roma, but eventually Heddwyn and her sisters. That solitary future made her shoulders slump.

"Keomi," Zin said, "I'm ready for our next step. Oriole isn't prepared for hers and Heddwyn's."

Why are you still talking about me? What about Heddwyn?

When she finally stole a peek at him, her heart raced faster. He stared at her with a directness she now craved a hundred times more than she feared. He also remained silent.

"We're offering Oriole a choice," Keomi said. "Others will not. My messenger has been sent. He cannot be recalled. Her uncle is coming for her."

"He's not my uncle," she grumbled. *He's also not what's unsettling me the most right now.*

Heddwyn's continued silence made her blood pound with trepidation. What was he thinking? Why didn't he speak?

Zin clasped Heddwyn's shoulder. "Our time together was brief but enlightening. If you had a choice, would you marry Oriole?"

"That's not a fair question." Not while they were trapped. "Heddwyn doesn't have to—"

"But I want to." The heat shining in his blue eyes enthralled her like an aurora in a dark land. "I want you to be safe."

The spell he'd cast vanished like a puff of smoke. She wanted more than being safe. She craved the things she'd never dared hope for. She wanted the same for Heddwyn.

"Marriage is the best way to keep Oriole safe. A husband's rights outweigh an uncle's or anyone's." Zin's proclamation coiled around her like a shackle.

Instinctively, she retreated a step.

"No, life is full of other ways." Heddwyn shook his head.

She did the same. "Do not lie to me or yourself. Marriage is binding. That's the rule of the law."

"But we can make our own rules." He bent his head and whispered close to her ear so that his words reached only her. "If our union isn't consummated, you'll be free to have it annulled whenever you wish."

She flinched. *I don't want that. Do you?* "You'd agree to such a thing?"

"To keep you free from Ulysses, yes."

"That doesn't sound like freedom."

"But it is a choice." His smile was gentle, but his eyes were determined.

"Are you making a proposal?"

"Yes, but I'm not doing it properly." He dropped to one knee. "Will you marry me? I vow to honor and protect you every day of my life, whether we..." He shrugged. "The rest can be as I said."

Her stomach turned hard. *I don't want a temporary arrangement. I want you forever.*

Heddwyn rose in a rush, and his words flowed just as fast. "It's too much to ask of you." He waved his hands in the air as he turned in a circle. "We'll find another solution. You don't have to marry anyone."

"But I will." She grabbed his hands and pulled him close again. "I will marry you." *Because I want to hold on to you for as long as I can. Because...I love you.*

CHAPTER 13

*L*ove was stunningly complicated.

Oriole now trusted Heddwyn completely, but she still couldn't depend on him to do what was best—for himself and thus for her. In this, he wasn't scatter-brained. He was steadfast. He'd always put others ahead of himself, but he deserved a future so much brighter than the one that awaited her.

Winter's dark was descending swiftly. The two weddings had happened even faster.

She'd followed Zin and Keomi's lead. She'd held Heddwyn's hand as they exchanged vows, then jumped a broom in a traditional ceremony around a campfire. She was now married to the man of her dreams.

She'd never been happier or more worried.

Only the young and the old had witnessed an event also devoid of music and dance. The rest of the Roma circled the camp, facing outward, rubbing their hands and stomping their feet to ward off frostbite. They stood on guard against something harsher than a January night.

The valley remained hushed as Heddwyn helped hitch her mare to her wagon.

Their luck had held. But they could travel only as far as the fading light allowed. Soon they'd make their own camp and share their first night as husband and wife. They might have only the one. She intended to make the most of it.

She'd share Heddwyn's bed tonight.

A pair of footsteps crunched the snow. Keomi and Zin had arrived for a final farewell.

Keomi held out the pistol her clan had taken from Oriole. "I wish you a long and prosperous marriage."

Oriole couldn't stifle her sigh. She'd grown to abhor lies.

"I speak the truth." Keomi continued waiting for Oriole to take Heddwyn's revolver.

She delayed reaching for the olive branch and instead focused on fastening the last harness buckle.

"But you haven't always been honest." Heddwyn's gaze was on Keomi, not her.

Oriole released another sigh. "I haven't either." She retrieved the handgun and stowed it by her rifle—now in its usual place under the blanket behind the driver's seat.

"You are more like your sister than you know," Zin said.

Keomi nodded. "One secretive. The other nearly silent. Both wily as foxes."

Look who's talking. The campfires behind the pair cast them in an unreliable light.

"Claptrap and twaddle," Heddwyn muttered as he boarded their wagon.

Was she any different? She wanted to be. She straightened her back. *I will be.*

"We'll find our truth on the trail." Heddwyn held the lines out for her.

She didn't hesitate to join him and accept what he

offered. She didn't know which direction they'd head, but she was eager to go. She raised her hands to snap the lines and begin the next stage of their journey together.

"Follow the sheep while their tracks still show." Keomi spoke so fast she rivaled Heddwyn's speed. "They may lead you to your sister."

Oriole's jaw dropped along with her hands. She clenched the lines in her lap, struggling not to let her hopes run wild. "How can sheep do that?"

"Only certain ones can," Keomi said. "With spiral horns and wool rumored to be as soft as snow."

"Merinos." Zin supplied the name Oriole had learned this morning. "I've seen them before. In my homeland."

And the Diaz family had them here. Or so Heddwyn had told her. A shudder shook her.

When Heddwyn's hand covered hers, she held on to him tightly.

Keomi looped her arm around Zin's. "We saw them when Wren was with us. Then again today."

But the shepherds had told her they hadn't seen her sister. Had Wren hidden in their flock? Had Wren, as Keomi said, been as *wily as a fox*? She'd have to be to disappear this long without being found by the number of people looking for her.

People like Lark and Oriole. And Mrs. Fitzgerald and the Llewellyn and Peregrine families. And Ulysses and his hired thugs.

"Wren used the sheep tracks to cover hers." She knew it in her bones.

Keomi nodded.

And after Wren hid in the Diaz flock, had she also hidden at their farm? Was she there now?

"We don't know where they go, but when herded, they always go in the same direction." Keomi pointed northeast.

A route she could've been heading long ago. And if she had, she might have found Wren days ago. Her sister wouldn't have suffered unknown hardships alone.

"Why didn't you tell me this before?"

Keomi's shrug spoke not of indifference but resignation. "Storms obliterated those first tracks, leaving nothing to follow. Poor luck for you, but good for Wren considering the man who calls himself your uncle could've been close by."

He'd be even closer now. He was coming for her. If she followed the sheep, she might find Wren. She might also lead Ulysses straight to her.

"I forgot to kiss my bride." Heddwyn turned toward her, blocking Keomi and Zin from her view as he lowered his head to hers.

She trembled for another reason now.

His lips didn't meet hers but skimmed her cheek. The stubble on his face tickled and tormented. After only a couple days away from his shaving tools, he'd developed a shiver-worthy start of a beard.

"Remember," he whispered close to her ear. "The Diaz farm is where I found Lark and Bryn's lambs. I'll take you straight there. We need not follow any tracks."

"Promise me you'll go to Wren. You'll find her and take her to Lark."

"Of course I will." Heddwyn's hand settled on her shoulder with an uncharacteristic weight. "We both will. We'll—"

Birdsong flitted around the circle of guards. Heddwyn pulled her flat against his chest. She strained to see around his reassuring but also blindingly wide bulk.

"Someone's seen my brother returning." Keomi scanned the Romani sentinels as if for a clue to where exactly.

Dread made Oriole's pulse pound. "Is Ulysses with him?"

Keomi's gaze fixed on a single point. "He's alone."

Relief surged through her, but not for long. Two guards half carried, half dragged someone toward them. A glimmer of firelight revealed the man who'd ridden away from her. Blood now covered his face.

"I found him." His words rasped as harshly as his breaths. "On the road. Like he knew I'd be there."

"Was a thin man with red hair with him?" Heddwyn asked.

"Yes."

Ulysses had been at the derelict homestead. Their paths had nearly crossed. How close had Heddwyn come to being beaten and bloodied? Or worse?

"I told him I'd found what he searched for but refused to say where. Not until he showed me the reward. He tried to whip the answer from me." He raised his hand to touch his brow, then winced and clutched his side instead. "But I escaped."

"He let you go." Oriole's own lash of truth made her flinch. "So he could follow you."

A screeching birdcall pierced the night. The ring of guards dropped like a wave, tumbling into the shadows. She tightened her hold on Heddwyn and dove sideways.

A gunshot punched his side of the wagon. The impact stole her breath. So did their fall.

Heddwyn held her close and rolled with her. They stopped with his back against the wagon wheel and his body between her and the shooter.

"Douse the fires and fetch my rifle," Zin hollered from the ground nearby.

She didn't mourn the loss of the light. Not with Heddwyn's arms still around her.

"I'm not here to hurt you. Not very much!" Ulysses' words rained down on them from the ridge. Then came his laughter.

"You expect us to believe that?" Zin yelled back.

"You *hurt* my brother!" Keomi shouted. "You shot at us."

"I was aiming for the Welshman. I still am." Ulysses' declaration made her hope for Heddwyn's future plummet.

"When you left him, how many men did he have?" Heddwyn's voice was low and determined. He sounded unafraid, which terrified her even more.

"Just the one," Keomi's brother replied.

"Olly olly oxen free!" Ulysses' laughter erupted again. "Playtime's over, little mice. Give me what's mine."

"He's gone mad." Keomi's summation was full of dread, and rightfully so.

Ulysses had often acted outrageously to gain what he wanted. He'd never cackled maniacally while doing so. His time in jail and on the run was unraveling a short tether to anything predictable. She feared being around him at the best of times. What would happen at his most depraved?

"The odds may never be better." Heddwyn released her and rose in a crouch. "I'll circle around them and—"

"No!" She yanked him back down. "Didn't you hear? He's aiming at you first. He's unhinged."

Heddwyn hovered beside her. When she leaned toward him, a length of cold steel blocked her. He'd let go of her so he could grab her rifle from the wagon seat. He now held a weapon instead of her.

"If I can get Ulysses back inside Denver's jail, you'll be

safe. So will this camp. And Wren and Lark. And my brothers and sister as well."

He'd mentioned everyone but himself.

"There's no other way. I have to do this. I have to go."

"Then I have to go with you."

"And what about Wren? You've never been closer to finding her."

She agreed. She also couldn't stop shaking her head. "You need someone to cover your back."

"I'll do it," Zin said.

"You can't." Keomi sounded as dismayed as Oriole felt. "Not after we just vowed to be unified. Your future is here with me."

"But our past is out there because of what we've done. And not done."

The couple's voices dropped to inaudible whispers.

Heddwyn's forehead lowered to touch hers. "The time for talk is over."

Regret constricted her chest. She'd wasted too much time refusing to speak to him. "If we can't talk now, I'll never see you again."

"Of course you will. Zin and I will capture Ulysses. I'll haul him to Denver. Griffin will guard the jailhouse while I come back to you."

He might succeed. Or he might die trying. She couldn't live with the latter. His plan was to leave. Hers was to save Wren and him. She had to let him go in order to do that.

"This is where we part ways." She'd said the same barely a few hours ago. It was a truth she couldn't dodge.

"No, I'm coming back for you." His tone was firm. "We're going to the Diaz farm."

She nodded. "One of us must make it there." *I'm going to make sure it's you.*

"Zin," a voice she hadn't heard before whispered from nearby. "I fetched your Winchester."

"Thank you." Zin's footsteps approached her—or rather, Heddwyn. "I'm ready. Are you?"

"No," Keomi objected.

"Yes." She found Keomi's hand in the gloom and held her still. "Let them go."

"Wait for me." Uncertainty roughened Heddwyn's voice. He suspected something.

Her heart seized with guilt, then joy. He knew her well now, *and* he still wanted to be with her. She'd never loved him more, but she couldn't tell him that. Not if she wanted to save him.

She sealed her lips and waited.

The instant Heddwyn was out of hearing distance, she asked Keomi to do one thing. She didn't wait for the woman's reply. She walked in the opposite direction Heddwyn had gone.

She fought her longing to run toward him instead. She focused on counting her strides and the seconds that passed. When she reached thirty, she also reached the edge of the camp. And she heard Keomi's voice. Right on time, doing what she'd asked.

"We're sending Oriole out," Keomi yelled. "Alone."

"Stop!" Heddwyn's cry boomed like cannon fire on a battlefield too far away to reach her.

She kept going. Deeper into the dark. Heddwyn's voice returned to where he'd last seen her before ricocheting wildly as he raced in search of her.

In a campsite covered in footprints, he couldn't tell which direction she'd gone. Keomi wouldn't tell him. Not if she wanted to keep Zin and her clan safe. Not if she wanted Oriole to leave and take Ulysses with her.

Oriole started humming a song one man would hear.

Familiar footsteps, heavy and deliberate, crunched the snow. Coming her way.

She stopped singing. She hadn't any breath to continue. She braced for hell. All the while longing for the sound of another man. Fast and impulsive. Her soul craved Heddwyn's approach

Instead, a sneering black-haired bully parted ways with the abyss.

"You'll pay for the grief you've caused me. Not to mention the money you stole." Her self-appointed uncle seized her arm and twisted it.

Tears flooded her eyes. She let them fall and glared with unrestrained abandon. "The devil take you. And me too, if need be."

Ulysses drew back but didn't loosen his grip. Surprise replaced his scowl. "Don't upset yourself. We'll collect your sister. You'll be easier to manage then."

"I haven't a clue where Wren is," she said, bluffing.

"Neither do I." His reply provided scant relief. He, like her, could be lying.

She gritted her teeth against any further comment, including reacting to his bruising hold.

"But we both know Lark's location." He dragged her through the snow in a zigzag path meant to muddle their tracks so no one could follow. "After I gather my men, we're heading straight to Songbird Junction."

CHAPTER 14

*H*eddwyn drove slower than he ever had. The only thing that moved fast was his eyes. Sitting on the edge of his seat, he scanned the road, the fields, the trees. He'd never stop looking for Oriole, but after many agonizingly long minutes scouring the dark around the Romani camp, he'd done as she'd asked.

He'd left her. He'd headed for the Diaz farm to find Wren.

Oriole had done what she thought was best for the Roma and for him. Returning to Ulysses would never be best for her, though. Especially now that she'd started speaking her mind. He prayed she'd go back to being the sweet-spoken liar.

Under Ulysses' iron fist, revealing the truth could be disastrous.

He exhaled a relieved but abrupt sigh when he finally reached the Diaz homestead. In the pale morning light, the sheep foraging on the winter grass between him and the buildings began bleating and scurrying.

Five people—one holding the reins of a saddled horse—

strode from the barn toward him. A lifetime together made their leader instantly recognizable.

Griffin carried someone small. Carefully, as if he held both glass and gold. His brother had found Wren.

All this time, I thought Oriole would be the one to find her. And I was just riding along to help. Now Griff's done the finding. And I'm just here to help him.

He raised his chin. *But soon I'll be with Oriole again. And I'll stay with her.*

He halted the wagon, spun on his seat to open the door behind him, then jumped down so his brother could climb up and take Wren inside. "How did you know she'd be here?"

"I didn't. I was making a delivery." As Griffin entered the wagon, he angled his head toward the couple now standing by Heddwyn. "When I arrived, Tino and this very kind lady took me straight to Wren. I'm forever in their debt."

"You owe us nothing." The young man clasped the hand of an equally young woman like she was a lifeline. He raised his other hand and held out the reins of Griffin's mount for Heddwyn to take. "We're just glad we could help."

While Heddwyn tied the horse to the back of the wagon, he took the opportunity to scan the people now clustered around the young couple like a protective herd. Behind them stood Tino's grandfather and two other men, also dressed in now familiar Diaz woolens.

"When I got home, I told Alafair—" Tino bit his lip before blurting, "I shouldn't have said your name."

Mr. Diaz patted his grandson's back. "Don't worry. We can trust the Llewellyns to keep a secret. And going forward, we'll say we informed *all of our family,* and then Wren was found."

Heddwyn finished securing the horse and rushed back

to the wagon's doorway to check on his brother's progress securing Wren inside. "Where did you find her?"

Tino raised his chin. "We—"

"No, just me. The details of my account may be important to Wren's recovery." Alafair's ominous tone halted Heddwyn in his tracks. "I was alone when I found her hiding in the sheep yesterday. She appeared worn out, as if she'd been there for days. When I told her I'd fetch help, her face lost its color. I imagine mine has done similar lately when questioning who to trust. I promised I'd return with only food and blankets. When I did, she hugged me but never said a word. And that's when I saw—" She inhaled sharply and clutched Tino's hand even tighter.

Tino drew Alafair closer so she could lean on him. "Wren has bruises around her throat. It looks as if she's been choked."

Wren hadn't been hurt when Oriole and Lark last saw her. Heddwyn's throat tightened with a terrible suspicion. Shortly before the three sisters fled Cheyenne, Ulysses had choked Lark. Not enough to leave many marks, but enough to leave her hoarse for many days. Was Ulysses also responsible for Wren's injuries?

Whoever her assailant had been, she'd managed to escape and stay away from him. Hiding in sheep. Hungry and hurting. With no help. Until Alafair found her.

His brother had been right all along. "Wren's stronger than I ever imagined."

Alafair nodded, then quickly shook her head. "But strength can't last forever. Last night when I went to check on Wren again, she wouldn't rise from her sleep. That's when I broke my promise to her. I told Tino, and we carried her inside and out of the cold."

Heddwyn's stomach rolled with apprehension as he

watched his brother carefully arrange the blankets over a still unmoving Wren on the bottom bunk.

"She'll wake up soon. She'll recover." Griffin spoke with a quiet certainty, but when he left Wren to stand in the wagon doorway, his face burned red and his tone rumbled with fury. "I should've come here sooner."

"Stop lashing yourself, Ruddy. You didn't know she was here," Heddwyn muttered as he struggled with his own self-reproach. He hadn't known either, but he'd received more clues than his brother had. Despite the shepherds' denials, he should've insisted on bringing Oriole here. But she wouldn't have agreed until after she'd visited the Roma. He turned in a circle, scanning the horizon, searching for—

"Peaceful! Did you hear me?"

"No," he replied to his brother's growled inquiry with equal heat.

Griff heaved a sigh. "I asked you where Oriole was."

He started pacing. The uselessness of that action made him throw his hands in the air. His impatience wasn't helping. "She was with me last night. We stopped at a Romani camp. Then Ulysses arrived, threatening to do his worst if we didn't hand over Oriole, so she left me again. Now she's with that devil and—"

"And once we get Wren to safety, you'll go find her *again*." Griff grabbed his arm and yanked hard. He hauled Heddwyn up to sit beside him on the driver's seat and shoved the lines into his hands.

Their light weight suddenly felt as heavy as chains. He longed to take Griff's horse and bolt in search of Oriole. But he'd promised her he'd find Wren *and* take her to Lark.

"I need you, brother. No one can get a wagon rolling like you. So, do what you do best. Drive fast. Get us to Songbird Junction."

Heddwyn did as he was told. They flew along the road. His brother went back inside the wagon to make sure Wren didn't fly out of her bed.

He braced his boots against the footboard and fixed his gaze on the curves in the road, guiding the mare to take each one at full speed. The sooner he got to Songbird Junction, the sooner he'd be able to unhitch the horse and ride even faster. And as soon as he left the junction, he'd be one step closer to finding Oriole.

CHAPTER 15

*B*eneath the evergreens near Songbird Junction's water tower, Oriole tripped and fell to her knees. Or had Ulysses pushed her? His hand on her shoulder held her down, while her heart leapt, then faltered. Her wagon sat beside Lark and Brynmor's cabin.

Heddwyn couldn't be here. She'd left him in order to save him.

"Drop back," Ulysses ordered one of his men. "Make sure no one sneaks up on us. The rest of you fan out in the trees behind the cabin. Wait for my signal."

Smoke drifted lazily from the chimney. Peaceful. Like Heddwyn's family's ironic nickname for him. This was now his brother's and her sister's permanent home and workplace. If the pair weren't outside, they were inside. And in need of a warning.

She tried to shout one. The handkerchief her dear old uncle had stuffed in her mouth stopped her. So did the rope he'd used to bind her hands behind her back.

She scanned the junction. The cabin, her wagon, the tracks, and the trees flanking them. Plus the shadows below their branches, including the one concealing her and Ulysses.

Heddwyn was nowhere to be seen. Neither was her mare. An unfamiliar horse dozed in the corral by the cabin. It probably belonged to Brynmor.

Heddwyn had driven in and ridden out. Fast. As usual.

Why had he come here? He should be looking for Wren at the Diaz farm. Her shoulders slumped. Wren hadn't been there, so he'd raced here to update Lark and Brynmor. She'd almost caught another glimpse of him.

Disappointment, then relief flooded her.

If she'd seen him again, he might have seen her. He wouldn't have left. He wouldn't be safely out of Ulysses' reach and still able to help Wren. He had a mission.

As did she. She had to help his brother and Lark.

Brynmor hadn't recovered from Ulysses' last attack. His gunshot wound was healing slowly, but the injury to his eye was permanent. If Ulysses came anywhere near Brynmor, Lark would put herself in danger to protect him. Brynmor would do the same for Lark.

I have to save them both.

First, she must free her hands. She twisted her wrists while trying to keep the rest of her body still, so Ulysses— and the man he'd ordered to guard his back—wouldn't notice and stop her.

Ulysses' gaze never strayed from his men preparing to attack the cabin.

Before he'd gagged her, she'd told them he couldn't pay them. He'd laughed and reminded them that as soon as they hauled her—and at least one of her sisters—back to Cheyenne, they'd be back in business. He could and would eventually pay them double if they did what he asked right now.

Their faces were familiar. His regulars from Cheyenne. Added to the scoundrel from the derelict homestead, his crew now totaled seven.

She was outnumbered. A familiar situation for her and Lark. When had the odds ever been in their favor?

She couldn't give up. She had to free her hands.

The rope chafed her skin. A wet trickle of blood dripped down her fingers. She gritted her teeth against the pain and kept rotating her wrists.

A train whistle echoed, approaching from the direction of Denver.

Ulysses' hold on her shoulder tightened. "Right on time."

He'd planned this? Of course he had. He was always scheming. After the train passed through Songbird Junction, it was bound for Noelle and then Cheyenne. Boarding it was the quickest way to get her and Lark to a location he could control.

The train chugged in and glided to a stop with its locomotive perfectly positioned beside the pumphouse and tower. The spout squeaked as it lowered to deliver water for the boiler.

Ulysses had chosen to hold her in the one spot hidden from the engine crew that still had a view of the cabin's door and the train's tail end. He'd also ordered his men to fan out on one side of the track. The side with the cabin.

They'd attack it, grab Lark, and drag her and Oriole onto the train and—

Ulysses' fingers dug into her shoulder like talons. Two men had disembarked from the last passenger car. Sheriff Guyette and his deputy, Nash.

"He's not supposed to be here," Ulysses muttered.

He'd said *he*, not *they*. Only one lawman was expected, was part of Ulysses' plan.

Which one? Would the other man help her? Probably not, but he might help someone like Brynmor. Her gaze flew to the cabin in search of him.

Lark stood in the open doorway.

No! Go back inside.

"Time to collect all that's mine." Ulysses raised his fingers to his lips to whistle his signal for the attack.

She threw herself flat on the ground so she could lift both feet. She kicked Ulysses in the shins. He fell beside her with a gasp and a grunt. She wrenched herself sideways, trying to roll away from him. And her hands finally broke free.

She tore the gag from her mouth and hollered an order for Lark and Ulysses' men. "Retreat! There are gunmen on the train."

Please believe my lie. If she wanted them to turn tail and leave, she must create a threat.

"Don't listen to—"

She ended Ulysses' countermand with another kick. This one to his stomach. She scrambled to her feet and ran away from him and the guard behind them. She darted around the pumping station, bearing away from the cabin.

Heaven strike me down if I ever lead him toward Lark.

She aimed for the gap between the back of the engine and the front of the coal car. If she could slip across the small platform linking the two, she'd be on the far side of the train. If she reached the trees on that side—

A bullet whizzed past her head. Splinters flew from the pumphouse wall as she ducked and turned in search of the shooter.

Sheriff Guyette crouched low as well. He also gaped at

her with disbelief. But not for long. He spun to face the man behind him.

His subordinate pointed his revolver at Oriole.

The iron flashed as Deputy Nash's arm swung sideways. He pistol-whipped his superior on the head. Then, his gun barrel raised once again to point at her.

Three shots popped like a chain of firecrackers. They hit the deputy, dropping him beside the sheriff.

Her gaze swept the junction. A trio of familiar shapes caught her eye. Lark shot from the cabin doorway, Griffin from her wagon's window, and Brynmor from behind the tail end of the train.

One of their enemies was down. *Run! Before the rest reach you.*

She bolted for the gap in the train.

Something caught her hair. Yanked her backward. Pain seared her scalp. An arm circled her throat, cutting off her scream and her air.

"You'll pay a hundred times for this." Using her as a shield, Ulysses pulled her toward the escape route she'd aimed to cross alone. He dragged her onto the platform.

The steam from the boiler beaded her face with sweat. The heat stole her breath. So did the sight of Heddwyn suddenly blocking their way.

Ulysses shoved her aside. A silver blade shone in his hand, arcing toward Heddwyn.

She grabbed the first thing her own hand touched. The shovel for adding coal to the boiler. The end glowed hot from having recently done that.

She whacked it against Ulysses' head.

His face turned red. He roared, stumbled, then lunged at Heddwyn again.

She scooped a shovelful of coal from the boiler and tossed it.

Her aim was true. She hit one side of Ulysses' face and neck, burning and melting his skin. His screams filled her ears as he fell forward. Blade still raised.

Heddwyn dodged left. His attacker toppled off the other side of the platform.

Ulysses rolled through the snow, making it sizzle and steam. His shrieks echoed in her ears. Nonstop.

"What have I done?" *Heaven forgive me. No one deserves that kind of pain.*

Ulysses crawled facedown through the snow, heading blindly for the trees.

Heddwyn drew her close to him. "Don't look. It can't be undone."

She buried her face against his chest and hid from the monstrous hurt she'd inflicted. She couldn't escape it. She'd do it again if it meant saving Heddwyn and Lark. "My sister—"

Her legs unexpectedly gave out beneath her.

Heddwyn's arms kept her upright. "They're at the cabin."

"They?"

"Yes, both Lark and Wren. I found her and Griff at the Diaz farm. I helped him bring her here. Then I almost rode off in search of you while you—" His lips pressed hard against her hair, and his voice turned urgent as he whispered, "Come to the cabin. Your sisters need you."

He knew what to say. He knew her well.

She rose to stand on her own. She'd always keep going for her sisters. And for Heddwyn.

Ulysses' cries faded into silence. But his vow from before —before she'd even dared to hurt him so horribly—rasped inside her head. *You'll pay a hundred times for this.*

If her actions didn't lead to his death, he'd return for her. As soon as he healed enough to stand upright, he'd extract his payment. From her. And anyone near her.

Heddwyn wasn't safe. After everything she'd done, she'd still have to leave him.

But first, she'd see her sisters and say a proper goodbye. Maybe she didn't have to go right away. She could stay for a day. Or two. Then it wouldn't hurt so much to leave.

So many little lies. She held on to them and Heddwyn, too.

CHAPTER 16

*F*ive days later, Oriole stepped down from another train at Songbird Junction. A regular occurrence of late, but not after today. *This was it. The last time.*

She had to stop clinging to the people she loved and to her lies. She had to let them all go. Her gaze immediately searched for Heddwyn. She didn't have to look far.

He stood with his brothers and Lark by the cabin. Wren was inside. She'd been there since Griffin had found her, and Heddwyn had found him, and they'd all come here. Robyn, Max, and Grandpa Gus had arrived soon after. The Llewellyn and Peregrine families kept rallying around each other.

Heddwyn wasn't the biggest or the oldest in his clan, but his gaze—staring directly back at Oriole—was the strongest. She could no longer look away. He drew her like a magnet.

Or a moth to a flame. Time to end everything with the truth.

She linked arms with the two old-timers who'd traveled with her from Denver. This time, she did the guiding. She steered Grandpa Gus and Mrs. Fitzgerald straight toward

Heddwyn, who waited by the cabin—or rather, by a faded red railcar parked near it.

"Was a tip-top notion," Gus remarked, "buying that caboose from the railroad 'n using a team of horses to get it off the tracks. In all my years hauling freight, never imagined doing that."

"Whose idea was it, then?" Mrs. Fitzgerald asked.

"Heddwyn's." Oriole's answer came with acceptance and appreciation for his continued meddling.

He couldn't stop trying to help her. It wasn't only her, though. It was her sisters, his brothers, and everyone around him. According to Lark, Heddwyn had said a caboose—with an interior converted to match Oriole's wagon's—would be the quickest way to increase the junction's living space.

Even for two, the one-room cabin was cramped.

Heddwyn had insisted that Lark and Brynmor needed their own space, and Oriole and Wren needed theirs as well. Only then could Songbird Junction be a home for all three sisters. And since Oriole enjoyed her wagon so much, Wren might like something similar.

Griffin had agreed. He'd also declared he'd be in charge of sprucing up Wren's railcar, while Brynmor continued managing the junction's freight, and Heddwyn went back to work in Denver. Since the caboose's arrival, Griffin hadn't left. He'd worked and slept here alone.

She and Heddwyn had done similar in Denver. He'd returned to his accommodations above Mrs. Fitzgerald's, while she spent her nights tossing and turning in her wagon parked behind the shop and her days in the shop, trying to distract herself by earning a wage in shopkeeping and instrument repair. So she'd have the funds to leave.

Just as soon as I tell everyone the truth.

Her mouth went dry as dirt when she stopped in front of

Heddwyn. His smile was encouraging as he tilted his head toward Lark. He knew her well. What she must reveal was hard enough to say to anyone, but Lark, having known her the second longest after Wren—who already knew this particular secret—deserved the truth first.

She spun to face Lark and blurted, "The violin isn't mine. It's Wren's."

Lark's dark eyes widened with shock, but not for long. "Wren brought the violin to the orphanage and gave it to you?"

Oriole nodded. "I only meant to hold it for a while. But after I admired it, Wren wouldn't take it back, so I just kept holding on to it."

"And that's important because—?" Mrs. Fitzgerald froze before her crown of white hair rocked with understanding. "Wren is my son's daughter."

Before she lost her gumption, Oriole rattled off the rest of her truths. "My mother didn't know who my father was. She said she couldn't even tell me who her parents were." Each admission made her stomach churn. "I don't know who I am. Not for sure. I'm not Irish or Cree or anything."

"None of that matters." Lark's tone was firm, but Oriole's world kept spinning.

She retreated a step. "But I don't have a clue who I am."

"Then it's a good thing I do." Heddwyn took her hand and halted her flight. "You're Lark's sister and Wren's too."

She shook her head. "I can't continue lying. I'm not related to anyone, even distantly. I'm not who I said I was."

Lark clasped her hand over Heddwyn's holding Oriole's. "And still I know you. In the most important ways."

"As do I," Heddwyn added with his familiar swiftness. "And that's because we've chosen to spend our time together."

"*And* now we're all here together again." Brynmor put his hand on top of Lark's.

Griffin added his hand to the pile. "*And* we should all stay together."

Heddwyn and his brothers formed a wall around her and Lark. Oriole's lips parted with astonishment because... she welcomed the arrangement. She wasn't trapped. She was included.

"Say goodbye to yer lies 'n yer past." Grandpa Gus elbowed his way in and added his hand.

Mrs. Fitzgerald did the same. "Excellent advice, Mr. Peregrine. The past is what we make of it. From now on, I'm choosing to call them all my granddaughters—and grandsons too." She winked at Gus. "These young folks need both of us to keep them on track."

Could it be that simple? Could a choice make the past no longer relevant?

Her hopes rose, then plummeted. "If Ulysses returns after what I did—"

"You gave him his comeuppance. Didn't he torch our barn?" A puzzled frown deepened the wrinkles on Gus' time-worn face. "Or am I rememberin' that wrong?"

"If he didn't do it, he hired the scum who did." Griffin drew back his arm with so much force that their hand pile toppled, leaving only Heddwyn's hand holding hers.

His touch remained steady but light, letting her know she could leave as well if she wanted. "Any one of us could've suffered Ulysses' fate, or worse, in the inferno he created."

"Don't forget that he also shot Brynmor." Lark put her arms around her husband. "And blinded him too."

"Only in one eye," Brynmor replied with a stoic snort.

He pulled Lark closer and kissed the top of her ebony hair. "I can still see my lovely wife, and that's what matters."

"Didn't he choke Lark and Wren too?" Gus asked.

Mrs. Fitzgerald's reply was grim. "He crushed Wren's voice."

Griffin's face flamed as red as his hair. He spoke in a low tone as if struggling not to shout. "Not permanently. She'll heal."

Would she? In Cheyenne, Ulysses had choked Lark in front of Oriole and Wren. To make a point. To keep their trio in line. But his increasing brutality had done the opposite. They'd finally run away. Lark's voice had been raspy for days, but Wren—who'd regained consciousness the morning after she'd been found—had yet to say even a single word.

Wren may've been notoriously quiet, but she'd never been completely silent.

Oriole's heart twisted with guilt and anger. She'd failed to protect her tiny sister. How hard had Ulysses choked Wren before she'd escaped him? Lark's bruises hadn't been nearly as many, or as dark, as the ones circling Wren's neck.

Like Wren's continued silence, the hush now surrounding Oriole became more and more disconcerting.

"What we're saying is—" Heddwyn scanned their group for the answer. When they remained quiet, he said, "You can make your home at Songbird Junction."

Same as the day they'd fought the fire in Denver, Mrs. Fitzgerald's elbow prodded Heddwyn in his side. "Say what's really on your mind, boyo."

His blue eyes blazed brighter than she'd ever seen. "If you go west, so will I."

She couldn't let him do that. "You're safer with your

family. We're—" She inhaled deeply with a rising conviction. "We're *all* safer together."

"It's always been this way," Lark said. "Wren knew it in Cheyenne. That's why she followed Robyn."

Wren followed Griffin as well.

She kept that revelation to herself. Wren's secrets were hers to reveal. As were Griffin's. The youngest Llewellyn brother's expression still appeared surly.

"What did you mean, Mrs. Fitzgerald," Gus asked, "when you told Heddwyn to say *what was really on his mind*?"

The flush on Griffin's face vanished as rapidly as it had appeared. He clasped Heddwyn's shoulder. "Leave it to a usually absentminded old-timer to keep you on track."

Heddwyn shrugged off his hold. "What matters is that Oriole is staying with us."

"Faith and begorrah." Mrs. Fitzgerald threw her hands in the air. "We've all seen how you both look at each other. You should be asking Oriole to stay *with you*. You should be proposing marriage."

Time to tell the rest of my truths. "He's already proposed."

The amazed gasps, sagging jaws, and wide-eyed stares suddenly erupted in a barrage of questions.

"When?"

"Where?"

"Why didn't you tell us?"

"Pipe down! Only one question matters." Gus doffed his flat cap and held it over his heart as if he stood in a chapel. "What did you say?"

"I said yes. We were married in a Romani camp."

Stunned silence returned until Gus asked, "Then why in tarnation are you still living apart?"

The frost on the branches sparkled with possibilities.

But the air remained still, as if holding its breath, like her, to hear what Heddwyn would say about their marriage. Would he bring up an annulment again?

He ran his hand over his hair, his neck, his now clean-shaven jaw. He did everything but speak to her.

She raised her chin defiantly. "I won't lie anymore."

"Speak now or forever hold your peace," Mrs. Fitzgerald urged. When Griffin snorted at the age-old line, the lady's shrewd-eyed gaze fixed on him. "Don't worry, *wee* boyo. I plan to give you plenty of advice as well."

When Griffin groaned, so did Heddwyn.

"Oriole." The huskily reverent but also deeply defiant way Heddwyn said her name made her quiver with anticipation. "I want you to have everything you've ever dreamed of, but I also need you to be safe. Your lies have protected you in the past. Remember, you kept saying you wanted to go west alone and—"

"That doesn't mean I want an annulment," she blurted. "I'll never want that."

He wrapped his arms around her and held her close. "I don't want one either. But you deserve to be free. And I want to stay with you forever." His words came quick. He hadn't changed. His unusual hesitation had vanished.

Thank the heavens and all of its lucky stars.

She hugged him back and hoped to never let go. "What's this talk of you and me? What happened to we?" she whispered before raising her voice for all to hear. "We want the same thing. The Roma married us, but we should have a..." She trailed off, wondering if they truly were finally in unison.

Heddwyn finished her sentence without hesitation. "A second ceremony with all of our family in attendance." When he leaned back to stare down at her, his unblinking regard heated her blood. "Then we need to make up for a lost wedding night."

"And after that?" Gus asked. "Where you gonna hang yer hats?"

"We could live in my wagon," she suggested.

Heddwyn nodded. "We've proven we don't need much space when we're together."

"Nonsense. The lodgings above my shop are a much better fit." Mrs. Fitzgerald's tone was firm.

A bark echoed as a black and white blur barreled out of the tree line, heading straight for her and Heddwyn. Happiness surged in her heart. She held tight to Heddwyn's hand as they both knelt to hold out one arm, so Little Fella could join them.

His wiggly little body fit perfectly into their combined embrace.

Mrs. Fitzgerald sighed. "I'm not keen on having a dog in my shop."

"But Mrs. Fitz—" Oriole shook her head. "But Grandmother dearest, you must reconsider."

Heddwyn nodded. "Little Fella is family now."

When they both rose to face the rest of their family, Oriole smiled at Lark and Brynmor, then frowned at the cabin where Wren was still ensconced. "We're needed here." Her gaze went to Mrs. Fitzgerald and Griffin. "But we're also needed in Denver." When she turned back to Heddwyn and rose on her tiptoes, he lowered his head so she could whisper in his ear. "We can't leave Griffin to handle the Denver freight alone. Look how he's frowning."

Heddwyn's younger brother's focus was now locked on the cabin.

"I think Griff's troubled by something other than work," Heddwyn whispered back.

She nodded. "He keeps getting left behind while everyone else jumps ahead to chase their dreams." When she settled back on her heels, Heddwyn raised his head.

Grinning like a brother who couldn't help but tease a sibling, he glanced at Griffin and said, "Oriole and I are staying in Denver, so you can—"

"I'm pitching my tent out here." Griffin gestured to the cabin and the caboose. "So *you and Oriole* can have the lodgings above Granny's shop to yourselves."

When Mrs. Fitzgerald opened her mouth to comment, Griffin cut her off. "Everyone needs their own space, *wee* Granny, including me. Oriole can continue working with you if she wants. Peaceful can run the Denver post and freight. I'm going after my own future."

"Just don't go charging off willy-nilly." Brynmor released one of his concerned-big-brother sighs. "We don't want you to disappear."

A muscle jumped in Griffin's jaw as he muttered, "But I will to get what I want. I'm gonna change everything." Stillness settled over his entire frame. His expression shuttered, exhibiting no emotion.

A prickle of unease crept up Oriole's spine. Wren had bonded with Griffin for a reason: for who he'd been in Cheyenne, not who he might become today or tomorrow. They all needed to pause and catch their breath before they took the next leap.

She drew Heddwyn away from everyone. Little Fella followed them, pressing close to their legs as he darted uncertain but also curious glances at the others.

When Gus leaned down and held out his hand, Little Fella began the long dance of approaching him cautiously. Gus didn't move. He waited patiently.

Little Fella, like all of them, was in excellent hands.

"Where are we going now?" Heddwyn raised a devilishly handsome eyebrow, and his tone turned teasing and enticing too. "Is it somewhere we can take advantage of being alone again?"

Oriole stopped when they were out of hearing distance of his and her families. Or now, more accurately, *their* families. "We're giving your brother the space he mentioned. At least for a little while. Because I know that my nosy husband can never stop interfering for long. And I'm fine with that." She laughed. "Actually, more than fine. I love you for it."

"I love you, too. Your stunning eyes. Your plucky spirit. Your ability to handle a wagon."

She laughed again and suspected she'd be doing a lot more. "That last part is important?"

"You've shown it can be. Like Bryn, I'm the luckiest of men to have a songbird bride in my life." His humor faded as his gaze went to Griffin.

Oriole nodded. She now knew Heddwyn as well as he knew her. In their lives, the time for pausing would always be short.

"Griffin will need all of our help if he wants to coax Wren back into his life." She set her palms on either side of Heddwyn's face and turned him back to look at her. "We need to get married again fast, then settle down even faster to help them."

Heddwyn's worry vanished in one of his heart-melting grins. "I like your pace, but what if we're tempted to tell a few fibs along the way to grease the wagon wheels?"

"So far, every day with you has been full of temptation." Oriole drew him closer so she could kiss him—in front of everyone and in the full light of day. "And as far as the future, whatever we do"—she promised against his lips— "we'll tackle it together."

Thanks for reading *A Bride for Heddwyn!* If you enjoyed the story, keep reading to see how writing a book review can make an author's day.

And if you're interested in reading Griffin and Wren's story, keep turning the pages until you reach *A Bride for Griffin's* excerpt following my Acknowledgments page.

DEAR READER

I hope you enjoyed Heddwyn and Oriole's journey to find a forever home in Denver—where they'll be close enough to visit their families regularly in Songbird Junction and (like Grandpa Gus and Mrs. Fitzgerald) they'll have many chances to continue helping (aka meddling in the lives of) their loved ones.

If you enjoyed this story, please consider posting a review online or email it to me at Jacqui@JacquiNelson.com

Every single review helps. No matter how long or short, they are a heartfelt gift that is sincerely appreciated. Hearing from readers makes my day and keeps me motivated to write my next book. I look forward to hearing from you!

You can review *A Bride for Heddwyn* on Amazon, Goodreads, or BookBub. Or even all three.

AMAZON
amazon.com/author/jacquinelson

GOODREADS
goodreads.com/jacquinelson

BOOKBUB
bookbub.com/authors/jacqui-nelson

ACKNOWLEDGMENTS

Thank you to all of my email list subscribers who've entered my character naming contests. In *A Bride for Heddwyn,* this included naming Sheriff Quincy Guyette and Deputy Nash.

Special thanks to...

- Janice Lachausse and Katrina Snow for choosing Nash
- Betty Vander Wier, Debbie Turner, Debby Guyette, and Liette Bougie for choosing Quincy
- Debby Guyette for having the last name Guyette!

In *A Bride for Heddwyn*, Sheriff Guyette's first name isn't mentioned, but it will be in *A Bride for Griffin* (Songbird Junction, book 3) where Sheriff Guyette will be leading a posse to capture Ulysses T. Stone. My sheriff will become a guide searching not only for a man but for his own redemption. So, when I searched online for the last name Guyette and discovered the following, I knew it was a sign to pick Debby's last name.

From SurnameDB, for the variant spelling of Guyet: In some instances the surname [Guyet] may be an occupational name for a guide, deriving from the Old French "gui", guide (a derivative of "gui(d)er", to guide). Job-descriptive surnames originally denoted the actual occupation of the namebearer, and later became hereditary.

If you'd like to subscribe to my email newsletter, visit my website JacquiNelson.com

A BRIDE FOR GRIFFIN - EXCERPT
Songbird Junction, Book 3

~

Can a sister who's lost her voice find harmony with the right man?

Singing with her sisters was Wren's refuge until they tried to flee their sadistic troupe manager, who retaliated by choking her until he crushed her voice. She only survived because a huge Welshman, with a personality as fiery as his red hair, taught her how to fight. She's dreamed of sharing a future with him—if she can alter his misconceptions about both of them. Can she convince him they belong together, or is she destined to a silent life alone?

Working with his two brothers to raise their younger sister was Griffin Llewellyn's purpose until all three of his siblings got married in the space of a month, leaving him alone to safeguard the woman he's dreamed of marrying. But he can't because she's lived a life of oppression, only asked for his help, and he's vowed to protect her from every threat, including himself. Can he save her from his temper and the violence that first fractured his family, or will he be her ultimate downfall?

CHAPTER 1

April 1878
Songbird Junction
On the train line between Denver and Noelle, Colorado

In the pre-dawn gloom shrouding Wren's caboose, recently hauled from the tracks and transformed into her home, a ghostly figure crouched by her bed.

A man's silhouette. Broad-shouldered. Big. But not big enough.

Her excitement turned to alarm. The man wasn't Griffin.

She bolted upright and aimed for his nose. Too late or too slow. Her punch fell short. Or swung wide. All impossible to tell with a target dodging so fast, but utterly predictable after being denied her sparring partner for two years.

Strength was earned, not given. Or so life had taught her. And kept teaching her.

Strong hands snared her wrists and held her captive. Her nightmare come true, with one difference. She wasn't in her ex-troupe manager Ulysses T. Stone's grasp.

"You've got grit, I know," the stranger muttered in a voice so low she struggled to decipher his words. "But you must leave this place. With me. Now. If you resist, he'll hear. And we both know what'll happen then. He'll defend you till his death."

A landslide of dread walloped her. The *he* could only be one person. Since January, she'd been blessed with a dozen defenders, but currently only one was in Songbird Junction.

Griffin Llewellyn.

A flood of work had taken his brothers and her sisters to Noelle or one of the other mountain settlements, leaving Griffin alone to tend the junction and her. A mute dependent who'd yet to help anyone in any real way. A disheartening fact that their combined families objected to mightily as a complete falsehood. Nonetheless, she was hellbent on changing, even if it meant she went to hell.

"Nod," her captor said, "if you want him to remain unharmed."

She nodded, then froze. He knew she couldn't speak. That's why he hadn't bothered to clamp his hand over her mouth. What else did he know about her?

When he spoke again, his tone lost all gruffness but remained hushed. "Be calm. Be still. And we'll evade his temper."

Her own temper flared. She hated when anyone labeled Griffin by his most fleeting of moods. He was a tireless guardian, a steadfast friend, and... Well, to her, he was so much more.

Two years ago, he'd been a patient tutor who'd shown her how to throw her first punch. Three months ago, his lessons had helped her escape Ulysses when that vile con-artist had been consumed by his own rage. But not before he'd choked her until he crushed her voice, the one talent that made her valuable to Ulysses or anyone else.

Griffin's teachings were the reason she was alive. He was also her biggest reason for not hiding in her caboose for the rest of her life. She wanted to see Griffin, to talk to him, to be near him always. But now she must leave him to protect him.

She nodded again. She could do this. She *would* do this. For Griffin.

Her captor's hold on her relaxed. "Until we've left this junction, I can't pull my punches away from him or any man. But I'll never hurt you."

She huffed in disagreement. If he or anyone hurt Griffin, her suffering would be endless.

Her captor huffed as well. Or had that been a chuckle?

"You're wise to withhold your trust and more than welcome to fight me later. Nod if you agree to that as well."

She did, keen to use everything Griffin had ever taught her. She wouldn't pull her punches either. Not after this man spoke so casually of laying his hands on Griffin.

"We've far to go, and it's raining." He released her and grabbed something from the floor. "Put this on." He handed her a coat.

Her coat. A fine woolen garment. Made to measure, just for her.

How had it gotten on the floor when she always hung it by the caboose's door?

The answer sent her thoughts careening down a new path. Her captor had taken the time to collect her coat before he approached her bed. This man did not act without forethought. He also wasn't completely heartless. He wanted to shield her from the rain and the cold.

Who on the ladder to hell was he? He wasn't a run-of-the-mill brute. She'd met plenty of those while performing with her sisters under Ulysses' rule in countless variety theaters and saloons.

He huffed again. That same contradictory mix of exasperation and amusement. Then he thrust her arms into her coat sleeves, as if she were the smallest of children who couldn't dress themselves. Next, he proceeded to put her boots on her feet.

This stranger was beyond strange. But he was still her abductor and, more importantly, a threat to Griffin. She restrained herself from kicking him but couldn't stop squinting into the dark, trying to see his face. Or at least his nose. A target prone to bleeding, which could be incredibly helpful for distracting an opponent. Or so Griffin had told her. And the one time that she'd struck Ulysses had shown her.

Was her abductor working for Ulysses? Did he plan to take her to him?

Even if she could sing again, her ex-troupe manager would always need more than her. He needed her sisters' musical talents as well. He craved the money and prestige that governing a songbird troupe had given him. But they hadn't seen Ulysses since January.

What if her decision to delay fighting this stranger put her sisters in danger? And eventually Griffin as well? What if they were captured and held captive? Or taken away, never to be seen again? Or injured, tortured, killed? The potentially horrific consequences of her actions or inaction pummeled and paralyzed her.

But beyond her...all remained calm. Except for the rain pelting the roof, the world outside her caboose was silent. The eye of the storm. A moment to seize.

Griffin was asleep in the loft of the recently built barn with its walls insulating him from her. Walls she'd previously longed to break down. But not now. Griffin must stay in Songbird Junction. And she must leave him here.

She gulped in a breath and lurched to her feet.

The stranger rose with her and picked her up. She landed belly down over his shoulder.

"Keep your head close to my back. The doorway is narrow. I do not wish to bruise you." His arm around her legs held her securely, but the concern conveyed in his words discombobulated her.

Their departure from her caboose was stealthily slow. Then came a jarring sprint and an equally abrupt halt.

Her abductor's hold on her tightened. He stood as if braced for a collision. "I'm not here to hurt anyone."

"But I am." The familiar voice was the one Wren craved to hear and be near, every minute since she started talking to its owner. Except for right now. Like a drowned dandelion wish, the lull in the storm vanished when Griffin said, "I'm gonna rip out your heart."

~

To read more about *A Bride for Griffin*, visit
JacquiNelson.com

If you haven't already, don't forget to add *A Bride for Griffin* to
your "want to read" shelf on Goodreads at
Goodreads.com/jacquinelson

SONGBIRD JUNCTION SERIES

The Llewellyn Brothers
Western Historical Romance Trilogy

Welcome to SONGBIRD JUNCTION, where Welsh meets West in Colorado, 1878. The journey to find a forever home and more starts here...

Brynmor, Heddwyn, and Griffin Llewellyn are three Welsh brothers bound by blood and a passion for hauling freight —in Denver, where hard work pays.

Lark, Oriole, and Wren are three Irish-Cree Métis sisters-of-the-heart bound by choice and a talent for singing—in any place that pays.

Will the frontier train stop of Songbird Junction be their families' salvation? Or their downfall when the sisters' troupe manager—a con artist who calls himself their uncle but cherishes only his own fame and fortune—demands a debt no one can pay?

Claim your ticket to travel from America's booming small-towns to the most promising train junction in the Rocky Mountains' snowbound wilderness where—during three perilous quests for freedom, truth, and harmony—the final destination will always be true love.

FREEDOM. TRUTH. HARMONY.

Bride for Brynmor - Book 1
Can a sister who's lived only for others find
freedom with one man?

A Bride for Heddwyn - Book 2
Can a sister who's lied to everyone find
truth with the wrong man?

A Bride for Griffin - Book 3
Can a sister who's lost her voice find
harmony with the right man?

PRAISE FOR THE NOELLE, CHRISTMAS STORIES...

The Calling Birds
Noelle, Colorado - Christmas 1876

"Jack and Birdie's story is suspenseful, romantic, sweet story of family, trust, love and survival. I couldn't put this story down!" ~ Carter and Conners Mom

"With secrets, outlaws, greed, and love this all provides for an amazing adventure." ~ Sandra S.

"An unforgettable read. Lovable characters, page turning plot, and satisfying resolution to all kinds of conflicts." ~ Deutsche OMA

"Birdie is a delight sassy woman who knows how to stand her ground...I loved the humor, the fear, the race against time" ~ Cyn

Robyn: A Christmas Bride
Noelle, Colorado - Christmas 1877

"The perfect book to set the mood for the Christmas spirit!" ~ Maria D.

"Beautiful story of friendship, love, and forever happy ever after." ~ Tonya L.

"I loved this book. It was revisiting old friends" ~ TJW

"Jacqui has hit a home run with this one!" ~ Peggy C.

THE CALLING BIRDS - EXCERPT
The Fourth Day in the
Twelve Days of Christmas Mail-Order Brides series

*A wanted woman's flight,
a man in pursuit of honesty, not stolen gold...
and only nine days left to save the town.*

Many years have passed since **Bernadette Bellamy** fled the Cariboo Gold Rush and her reputation as the sister of a French-Canadian gang of thieves. Armed with only an honest talent for sewing and a willingness to lead a solitary life on the run, she stays one step ahead of everyone seeking her brothers' last—and now lost—heist. Until a craving to settle down makes her reinvent herself as **Birdie Bell**, a dress shop owner. The arrival of an old foe combined with her desire to hold onto her treasure trove of fabrics has Birdie joining a wagonload of brides bound for a remote town.

After losing his leg and his wife, **Jack Peregrine** buries his pain under a mountain-high pile of work. He only agrees to sign up for a mail-order bride to save the town of Noelle, keep his freighting business, and care for his absentminded grandfather. But Jack's request for a sturdy bride who won't crumble under his burdens brings him a woman as tiny as she is troubled. Can two mismatched people band together to become the perfect match?

THE CALLING BIRDS

Noelle, Colorado
December 24, 1876

A crowd of women filled *La Maison's* front hall. One of them was Jack's bride, Birdie Bell. A hard-working woman who'd started her own dressmaking business in Denver. A mature woman of thirty. A strong woman who wouldn't break under life's hardships.

Maybe his luck would change today. With time Miss Bell might come to respect or maybe even enjoy his company. He needed this marriage to last.

He should've looked for his grandfather first, but he couldn't stop his gaze from scanning the women in search of his bride. Even wild-swept from the storm and huddled together shivering from the cold, the women were a fine-looking bunch. How had Mrs. Walters managed that?

A raven-haired, pale-skinned woman standing slightly apart from the rest snared his attention. Her beauty would've been enough to hold any man spellbound, but her tiny size turned him rigid with concern. A woman so small wouldn't last long in a town like Noelle.

His worry turned to anger. Whoever had asked her to come here should be horsewhipped!

A faint smile curved her mouth, as if she was amused by the prospect of being housed in a location as scandalous as La Maison. He must be dreaming. She shouldn't be here, and she couldn't be amused.

She surveyed the room, studying everything and everyone—until she saw him. Then she stared at him the way he felt he must be staring at her, as if mesmerized.

"I've come for a bride," a voice proclaimed loudly, a familiar voice that made him cringe. "Which one of you is the future Mrs. Peregrine?"

The woman spun to face the speaker—his Grandpa Gus.

A wave of gasps and tittering laughter swept through the crowd. Several of the women glanced at the tiny woman who'd captivated him. She was now staring at Gus with wide eyes.

Her gaze darted to him. When she caught him still staring at her, her expression turned blank and devoid of emotion. She straightened her shoulders, strode straight up to Gus, and said in a lyrical voice with a seductively foreign accent, "I am the bride you seek, Mr. Peregrine. My name is Birdie Bell."

A surge of euphoria followed quickly by alarm made him stagger and lean heavily against the nearest wall. This tiny Frenchwoman couldn't be Miss Bell. He'd asked for a strong woman. This one wouldn't be able to hold up under his workload, the rough town, or the surrounding wilderness. She'd abandon Noelle and him.

Could he blame her if she did?

If she didn't, she might die here.

"No!" His voice shot out louder than Gus' a moment ago.

Complete silence descended around him. The chance to make a good impression was long gone. Everyone in the front hall stared at him, including his tiny bride.

To read more about *The Calling Birds*, visit JacquiNelson.com

If you haven't already, don't forget to add *The Calling Birds* to your "want to read" shelf on Goodreads at Goodreads.com/jacquinelson

Deadwood, Dakota Territory 1876...
In a gold rush storm, can an unlikely pair rescue each other?
Raven wants to save one person. Charlie wants to save the
world. Their warring nations thrust them together but duty
pulled them apart—until their paths crossed again in
Deadwood for a fight for love.

EXCERPT
RESCUING RAVEN - CHAPTER 1

Fighting a growing impatience fueled by rage, Charlie
Jennings drew his revolver and urged his horse through the
trees flanking the Deadwood Trail. Below him, an
Appaloosa with the strikingly similar color of his own horse
—white covered from head to hock in chestnut spots—was
rein-tied to the back of a buckboard. If the horse hadn't
caught his attention, he might not have given the transport a
second look.

He might not have seen her.

The wagon rattled forward carrying one silent and seven
grumbling passengers. When a bend in the trail cast the sun
in the eyes of the guards, one riding behind and the other in
front, he charged his spotted mare down onto the road.

Everyone in the wagon, except for the cowering raven-
haired woman, screamed. The driver jerked on the reins.

The horses skidded to a halt. The guards scrambled for their weapons.

The click of his revolver being cocked made them all freeze.

The silence that followed was as heated as the summer sun on his back. The guards glared at him through squinted eyes. He kept his focus on them as well—lined up in a neat row down the barrel of his Colt Peacemaker.

"Jennings," growled the closest man, who went by the name Big Bill. "You shouldn't be here."

"Yeah," hollered Bill's partner, a stranger who resembled a beanpole.

Frontier trails and towns had a way of attracting similarly named men, including the Charlies like him. They also had a fondness for embellishment. The deck was stacked in favor of the rear guard being called Skinny Sam or Loud-mouth Pete.

"We heard you were guidin' a miner 'n his four kids, the ones who lost their ma, away from Deadwood." At least Skinny hadn't heard, and used, the double-barreled moniker Charlie had been saddled with since arriving in the Black Hills.

"But you," he shot back, "didn't hear that my job finished ahead of schedule."

"Well," Bill said on a long breath, "ain't that a spot of bad luck."

"Not for one of your passengers." He didn't look her way. He'd already seen enough: a ragtag assortment of women, one hunched with her dark head over her wrists tied to the wagon.

To read the rest of *Rescuing Raven*, visit my website JacquiNelson.com and sign up for my newsletter.

ALSO BY JACQUI NELSON

SONGBIRD JUNCTION SERIES

A Bride for Brynmor - Book 1

A Bride for Heddwyn - Book 2

A Bride for Griffin - Book 3

The Llewellyn Brothers and Songbird Sisters trilogy is set in Colorado, 1878, and feature characters from my two Noelle, Colorado, Christmas stories.

∾

NOELLE, COLORADO

The Calling Birds: The Fourth Day - Christmas, 1876

Featuring characters from *Choosing Bravery*

Robyn: A Christmas Bride - Christmas, *1877*

Featuring characters from *The Calling Birds*

∾

LONESOME HEARTS SERIES

Between Heaven & Hell - Book 1, Oregon Trail, 1850

Following Faith - Book 2, Oregon, 1852

Choosing Bravery - Book 3, Oregon, 1868

Rescuing Raven - Deadwood, 1876, a FREE read for

my newsletter subscribers

∾

GAMBLING HEART SERIES

Between Love & Lies - Book 1, Dodge City, 1877

Between Home & Heartbreak - Book 2, Texas, 1879

∿

STEAM! ROMANCE AND RAILS

Adella's Enemy - Kansas, 1870

∿

To learn more about my books, visit my website

JacquiNelson.com

ABOUT THE AUTHOR

Fall in love with a new Old West... where the men are steadfast and the women are adventurous. You'll find Wild West scouts, spies, cardsharps, wilderness guides, and trick-riding superstars in my stories. Those are my heroines. Wait till you meet my heroes!

My love for historical romance adventures with grit and passion came from watching Western movies while growing up on a cattle farm in northern Canada. I've been nominated for over 20 awards and won the RWA® Golden Heart® & the Laramie® — but my best reward is hearing from readers who have enjoyed my stories.

Email me at Jacqui@JacquiNelson.com

For updates on giveaways, special events, and more, join my newsletter at JacquiNelson.com amazon.com/Jacqui-Nelson/e/B00EE6GE88

goodreads.com/JacquiNelson

bookbub.com/authors/jacqui-nelson

facebook.com/JacquiNelsonAuthor

instagram.com/jacquinelsonauthor

pinterest.com/JacquiAuthor

x.com/Jacqui_Nelson

youtube.com/@jacquinelsonauthor

tiktok.com/@jacquinelsonauthor